D0340863

THE SECRET DEEP

The Secret Deep

LINDSAY GALVIN

Chicken House
Scholastic Inc. / New York

First published in the United Kingdom in 2018 by Chicken House, 2 Palmer Street, Frome, Somerset BA11 1DS.

Library of Congress Cataloging-in-Publication Data available

ISBN 978-1-338-56739-7

10 9 8 7 6 5 4 3 2 1 20 21 22 23 24

Printed in the U.S.A. 23

First edition, February 2020

Book design by Maeve Norton

For my Sea Boys, Edward and Oscar

What are deep? The ocean and truth.

CHRISTINA ROSSETTI

PART ONE
STRANDED

NOW

I'm not dead.

But I'm . . .

not breathing.

Chest shudders, heaving. Panic pushes me back down into darkness.

I float up toward light.

wisps of thought . . .

can't catch . . .

Noise. Booming, rhythmic.

Light. Color.

Chest full, swollen, something inside—doesn't belong.

Body flips over, out of control, heaving chest—in and out. Hot liquid gushes out of me, again and again and again. Splutters, gasps, soreness in my throat.

Whistling in and out.

Air.

My thoughts stutter. Warm relief. Confusion.

Something happened to me. I've forgotten, I've been—my brain is—hurt.

I can't see.

Solid surface beneath my shoulder, hip, ear. I lie on my side panting, mind trying to grasp on to—I can't remember.

I'm so heavy, so sleepy . . .

Come on, think. I'm alive, that's a start. There's a problem with my memory.

My eyes want to blink, but there's something over my eyelids. I raise myself on one elbow, fumble and peel off sticky patches, wincing at the drag on my lashes.

Blinding light. My hand springs up, shielding, then I narrow my eyes as they get used to the glare. The swishing sound is constant; I have heard it before.

My breath catches, and when I cough there's a bittersweet taste in my mouth.

Head too heavy for my neck, I narrow my eyes. Sparkling white below, hot blue above, and turquoise in front . . .

Sand. Sky. Sea.

Beach.

I'm on a . . . beach.

Alone? It's too bright, I can't see any distance, can't see any . . . one.

I'm alive and that's a surprise. I can't remember why. *Track back*. What is the last thing—?

Cool whiteness.

Memories spool into my mind.

The mist. My hand on the door handle, frantic twisting. It wouldn't open.

Poppy. She was in my arms. Blood rushes in my ears, throbs at my temples.

Where is my sister?

I pull myself into a kneeling position.

"Poppy!" My cracked whisper is swallowed by the soft scrape of the sea.

BEFORE

1

Poppy peers out of the plane window, nose pressed against the glass, and I follow her gaze. Dark, lush-looking forest reaches to the coast, where it bites into a sea of shining metal.

"I'm starving," she says.

"We just had breakfast, and you left half of it."

"I wasn't hungry then."

"That figures." There are no refreshments on this flight as

it's only an hour long. I rummage in my backpack. "Well, I've got apples and a banana . . . oh."

I hold up the banana, split and oozing brown mush all over the apples. We pull identical faces of disgust, but my laugh feels hollow. If Mom were here, there'd be more than enough snacks for this epic journey, plastic boxes of pasta salad and chocolate brownies we'd made together.

I look across the plane aisle at Alison, the flight attendant traveling with us. I'm thirteen, so I could fly alone, but Poppy is eleven and an unaccompanied minor, so she needs an escort. Alison met us at Heathrow and is as quiet and as organized as her smooth helmet of hair suggests, getting us through the connections at Los Angeles and Auckland much more easily than I ever could have. She's not listening to Poppy's appeal for food now, intent on her phone. I wonder how much my aunt paid for her to come all this way, guiding us through two airports, two twelve-hour flights, and onto this final plane.

There's a rustle from the seat behind us, and a sharing-size packet of chips dangles above Poppy's head.

I turn to look through the gap between the headrests and see a boy around my age failing to blow a strand of damp blond hair out of his eyes. I noticed him when we boarded, as he was soaked through. It was raining in Auckland; apparently it does that a lot on the North Island of New Zealand. At least the weather will make us feel at home.

"Nice. Thanks," says Poppy, taking the chips. She turns to me, eyebrows raised, and when I realize she's checking if I'm all right with this, I shrug. She's two years younger, but I'm not used to being in charge.

Poppy opens the chips and kneels on the seat, facing backward to talk to the boy.

"I'm Poppy, and this is my sister, Aster. So where are you going?"

"I live in Gisborne," says the boy. "I've been visiting my rellies in Auckland, now I'm off home."

"Rellies?" says Poppy, a laugh in her voice. The boy's accent is broad New Zealander, every sentence ending on a question.

I try to surreptitiously elbow Poppy. "Relatives," I whisper.

"I know, I just didn't know people actually speak like that," she says, grinning at him. He smiles back, then pulls a fake serious face.

"Well, I didn't know people actually spoke like *you*. How do you do?" he says in what I guess is supposed to be a posh English accent and sounds nothing like us, as we are from East London.

Poppy bursts out laughing, spraying chips. Within the next few minutes she finds out his name is Sam, he's fourteen, his favorite food is nachos, his favorite color is orange, and he likes mountain biking.

Then she tells Sam I'm a champion swimmer.

"All right, Pops, slight exaggeration," I say. I rest my cheek against the headrest and catch the boy's eye through the gap so I can raise my eyebrows in apology for my blabbermouth sister.

"Only being friendly," says Poppy, "unlike you. Anyway, you *are* a champion, you set that record and won that big cup—"

"That was two years ago and only regionals . . ." I trail off, feeling exposed and embarrassed for explaining it.

"To be fair, that does sound like champion-type stuff," says Sam. There's a dent in one cheek where he's suppressing a smile, and I narrow my eyes at him, finding myself smiling back, just a bit.

"Yeah. See?" says Poppy.

"So are you taking a vacation?" he says, directly to me. I swallow. Now, when I'd rather she did the talking, Poppy is giving serious attention to the chips.

The pause is almost long enough to be awkward.

"We're going to live here in Gisborne with our aunt, Iona. Our mom died a few months ago. Cancer," I say quickly; the words come out quiet but feel too large for my throat.

"Crap. Sorry." He pauses and swallows. I look down. When he continues, his voice is low.

"My granda has the same, he's doing OK right now."

When I meet his eyes again, I see his cheeks are pink and feel heat spread across my own face and throat. No one who has someone they love in cancer treatment wants to hear or speak about death. I wish I could think of something else to say.

"He might recover, loads of people do," says Poppy, screwing up the empty chip packet, oblivious to the change in atmosphere. "We are orphans—Mom and Dad broke up when I was a baby and he died in a car accident."

The boy's eyebrows climb higher. He's looking from Poppy to me like we have the worst luck ever. Poppy continues quickly.

"But Iona is Mom's younger sister, and she's awesome."

I turn back around, listening to Poppy describe how Iona is an oncologist—a cancer doctor—who works all over the world, from war zones to remote jungles. She doesn't mention that we've barely seen our aunt in years, or that when Mom was dying of cancer, she was out of contact, treating cancer in others.

The boy shows Poppy some mountain biking videos on his tablet. She insists he takes a selfie of all three of us with her phone, directing him how to hold it and then dragging me into the shot, her skinny arm around my neck as he leans over the backs of our seats. Eventually Poppy settles back and plays a game on her phone, and it isn't long before a voice announces that we are preparing for landing at Gisborne: local time nine a.m., the weather cloudy with showers, and the temperature sixty-eight degrees. January is English winter, New Zealand summer. Our escort, Alison, checks that we both have our lap belts fastened, and I screw my eyes tight for the landing, like I always do, feeling my heart rise in my throat. The touchdown is a little bumpy but not too bad.

Poppy presses both hands against the window. Her hair is much blonder at the ends than at the roots and is in two messy French braids. The part is wonky where she's getting used to braiding them herself, rather than bossily directing Mom on how she wants them each morning.

I chew my lip. New Zealand is such a long way to come—we've never even visited, and now we are moving here. But it's where Iona lives, and without her it would be a foster placement for Poppy and me. Social services would try to keep us together, but what if that didn't work out? I can't even think about being away from Poppy. We were the only family at Mom's funeral, and it was the first time in our lives that our lack of relatives became an important thing. We stayed with Mom's best friend for nearly a month before social services finally tracked Iona down and she called, horrified she'd not been there for Mom or us. I realized later that Mom never told her sister how bad it had gotten. It took another two months for Iona to organize our flights to New Zealand.

My eyes follow a single drop of condensation, trapped between the two layers of glass in the plane window, powerless in its course. Like us.

Alison ushers us off the plane and across the tarmac to the small, low building of the regional airport. She locates our luggage and leads us through to arrivals, where there are a few people at the barrier but no Iona. Sam is a few paces in front of us, and he turns.

"Give me a buzz if you like," he says. "Happy to show you around."

"OK. Put in your number," says Poppy. Sam takes her phone, taps the screen, then strides off with a smile and a wave.

"She's there!" says Poppy, pointing. "Oh—she looks even more like Mom now."

Iona is on the other side of the revolving doors—she hasn't spotted us yet. I hardly recognize her and see that it's her lack of hair that makes her look so like Mom did toward the end. Last time we saw Iona, she'd worn her long cornrow braids tied back in a knot; now her hair is closely cropped against her head. My heart trips. Mom's spiraling curls had been her trademark, and although she made light of it at the time, it had been a huge thing for her when she lost her hair to the chemo. I lean into Poppy for a moment and feel her bony shoulder against my arm, solid.

Iona's eyes crinkle at the corners as she finally spots us.

Poppy gives Iona one of her stiff tight hugs, and Iona's eyes squeeze shut as she hugs her back. A couple of years ago I would have hugged her too, but now I'm closed up, remembering Mom's hospital bed and the funeral, when having Iona there would have lifted the burden.

"I am so pleased to see you. Hope the journey wasn't awful?" she says.

"Not too bad, thanks," I say, burrowing my hands in my pockets. Poppy starts chatting, and I get used to seeing Mom's sister again. Iona is taller than Mom, her figure rounded and strong-looking. Her mouth is like mine and Mom's, full and wide, slow to smile. Same eyes as Poppy, deep-set and almost maroon-brown with curling lashes. I have deep golden-brown skin like Mom's, but Iona's is lighter. Our dad was white, and Mom and Iona are half African American, half Korean. We never knew our grandparents; they met while traveling and were both doctors who worked abroad, like Iona. My grandmother died young, also of cancer. Guess we really aren't a very lucky family.

I raise my chin. Mom adored Iona. Mom's sister might not have been there for us before, but she's here now.

We say goodbye to Alison, and Iona takes our bags and heads out of the airport and across the parking lot. We pile into the back of her dusty red pickup.

I'm surprised when we drive out of the small low-slung city of Gisborne, but I figure Iona's house must be in the suburbs. The road is quiet and straight. The clouds part, and the tarmac ahead gently steams in the watery sun. We drive on, passing a few small towns on the way, cutting through thick forest, then green hills with the sea in the distance to our right. Just as I'm about to question how far outside the city we are, Iona pulls up onto the curb beside the road. She draws a deep breath and turns.

"I've been a bit disorganized." She pauses, looking pained, then lays her hand over her heart. "I hope you can forgive me."

I meet Iona's eyes for the first time, and my heart leaps into my throat. She can't have changed her mind about being our guardian, not after flying us all the way out here.

"I have a tenant in my house while I work on a project nearby. I didn't realize my contract with them is for another few weeks. I wondered how you two would feel about spending a bit of time with me out at my fieldwork site? There's plenty to do, it's an ecovillage in the proper bush."

I lean back against the seat.

"You mean go there . . . now?" I say.

She nods.

"Are we camping?" I turn and see Poppy's eyes narrowing. "Don't you work at a hospital? I thought you were a cancer doctor."

I swallow. No house for a couple of weeks. I'd been looking forward to lying on the bed in my new room, listening to music. Closing the door and my eyes.

Iona smiles.

"I am a doctor, Poppy, but I'm also involved in medical research. I've been working with a group of students studying the health benefits of early human cultures. Would you be willing to try it for a few days? If you don't like it, we'll book into a hotel until the house is ready."

"How far is it?" I ask.

"We can be there by midafternoon if we leave now," she says. Iona meets my eyes. Her gaze is very steady, and I look down at my hand, picking at a loose thread on the seam of my jeans. I remember the last time Iona visited—the four of us had played cards late into the night, laughing so loudly the old man in the flat upstairs had banged his walking stick on the floor.

Iona is Mom's sister. This will be fine. I feel Poppy looking at me, but I don't catch her eye.

"OK, then," I say.

Iona drives on, and I stew in sudden anxiety. She sent us photos of a three-bedroom house by the river. She told social services that's where we'd be, and our social worker said she'd contacted family services in New Zealand so I could continue my therapy. My shoulders are so tense it hurts; I'm wound tight all the time. But plans change, and I need to be able to deal with that. Being here, looked after by family, will help me deal with everything.

After another fifteen minutes or so, I hear the *tick tick tick* of the turn signal. The turnoff is barely visible, just before a sign saying Tokomaru Bay.

Poppy snaps a photo of the sign on her phone.

Now she's texting Sam—the boy from the plane—underneath the hoodie on her lap so Iona can't see what she's doing in the rearview mirror. She must have picked up a local phone signal. I frown and peer over her shoulder. Beneath the photo of the road sign she's written:

> Staying at ecovillage camp thing. Poppy from the plane X

He replies right away.

> Cool. I sometimes ride the trails out there. Catch you in town sometime. Sam.

2

We're in the truck for nearly another hour, bumping at high speed, first over a bone-rattling track, then across rolling hills that seem to have no tracks at all. Iona talks, and we listen. She tells us that this area has a mainly Māori population, but the ecovillage is between Māori land and the national park, in a small patch of untouched forest that leads to the coast. We finally jolt to a halt behind a cluster of low trees. The sun is now high. The time difference has left me disoriented. It's past mid-day now, but I feel like the day has been going on forever.

Just through the trees beyond the truck is a shiny green quad bike with thick-tread tires, parked half-concealed in the bushes. Iona strides over to it and lays her hand on the hood. She gives her head a little shake, her forehead creased.

"Everything OK?" I ask.

"Oh yes, fine. We walk from here," says Iona, shaping her expression into a smile and talking briskly. "We'll come back for the big luggage—it will be safe in the truck—so just pack what you need for a few nights. Oh—and wear your hiking boots."

We do as she says, throwing toiletries and clothes into our small backpacks, changing our shoes for the boots Iona sent us the money to buy. As we follow her along the path, I glance back at the quad bike and wonder why it made Iona look so unsettled.

It is midafternoon when the path ends. Poppy has just started whispering that she has a blister, and my feet feel hot and swollen in the new boots.

"Welcome to Wildhaven," says Iona.

I hadn't seen the green chain-link fence in the gloom and would have walked straight into it. I hook my fingers through the wires; it's about ten feet tall, and the top slopes outward, the opposite direction from animal enclosures at the zoo, designed to keep things out rather than in. Iona presses her thumb against a small black panel, and a green light flashes.

Poppy tugs my arm, whispering in my ear, "What sort of student camp is this?"

The door swings open, inward. Iona meets my eyes with a reassuring smile. "Hiking and mountain biking are popular in the national park, and with patchy GPS it's possible to wander far offtrack. It's important the study isn't disturbed," she says quickly. "You have both been amazing. I never really noticed how far it was—I'm usually alone on supply runs."

"So what exactly is this ecovillage? Tents?" says Poppy, hesitating in front of the gate.

Iona shakes her head with a smile. "No—all wooden huts, we only use natural materials. Don't worry, it's very comfortable, just set up without any technology."

Poppy narrows her eyes. "By technology you mean phones and stuff?"

"Phones, computers, TV. There's nothing digital. We don't have any electricity at Wildhaven."

I'm thirsty, and my head pounds. Poppy grips my arm, widening her eyes in a questioning look. And she's right, this is a bit strange. But it's a relief to follow Iona, to not have to think about what's best for both Poppy and me anymore.

A fresh breeze blows through the trees, lifting the escaped curls from my neck.

"Are we near the sea?" I ask.

"Oh yes. Only around half a kilometer."

Poppy loves the beach, and I feel her hand on my arm relax a little as I step through the gate, pulling her along with me. As Iona closes it behind us, Poppy slips her phone into the waistband of her jeans, hidden.

We continue along an upward-sloping path through the trees. As we reach the top of a ridge, the ecovillage appears below us, nestled in a natural hollow at the base of a valley, surrounded by thick forest. I catch a sparkle of sea over the trees at the far side. Below in Wildhaven, wood cabins are clustered around a larger circular shelter, and I smell woodsmoke in the air. I hear voices and the steady tapping of a tool. My eyes shift to the side of Iona's face. Her head is tilted, her bottom lip caught between her teeth. There is something strangely intense about her expression.

A group of students races past us as we make our way down the hill. There are five of them, two boys and three girls, and they call out a greeting to Iona as they run by. I catch a waft of fresh sweat.

"They aren't wearing shoes, doesn't that hurt their feet?" says Poppy. I hadn't noticed.

"You'd be surprised how quickly the soles of the feet harden," says Iona. She pulls off her own boots and stuffs her socks inside. She shows Poppy the underside of a strong-looking foot, pointing out leathery pads of skin.

"See?" She grins at Poppy, who smiles back, but as soon as Iona's back is turned, her smile morphs into a comedic grimace aimed at me. I shake my head at her. When we enter the camp, the students smile their greetings.

"We're not into awkward introductions here, you'll soon get to know people," says Iona.

My heart contracts as I am reminded strongly of Mom, who hated anything fake. She never encouraged us to smile when we didn't feel like it or hug each other to make up if we didn't want to. I distract myself from the lump in my throat by focusing on what I see. There are around fifteen young people, somehow fewer than I was expecting. The students are dressed mostly in battered-looking jeans and hiking boots, although some are barefoot. A lot of them wear tops in plain dark-green fabric in various stages of fading, and some have leaves and leather decorations in their hair and around their wrists. One girl wears a crown of flowers. Seems like every shade of skin color is represented here. Inside the central shelter a group is weaving grass; others are chopping vegetables into a large cooking pot or sitting cross-legged on mats and carving wood with various tools. Iona stops to talk to a girl bringing in a basket of leaves and flowers, and Poppy and I linger next to a boy who gazes at me curiously as he scrapes a knife back and forth over a portion of animal skin, shaving off the flesh with reddened hands. He has warm brown skin and light eyes beneath thick black brows. I catch a metallic whiff of blood and when I wrinkle my nose, he copies the gesture.

"You can help if you like," he says. His accent is strong, not local.

"Not really our thing. No offense," says Poppy. The boy smiles, and I realize that despite the strength in his arms, he doesn't look much older than I am. When I smile back, he winks at me like he's my granddad or something. I want to ask if he has something in his eye, but instead I shoot him a scornful look. Iona is back.

"So are the students from a local college?" I say.

"Yes, most are international students," says Iona, now striding ahead. I remember what she said before, that she's working on a study of healthy lifestyles.

Beyond the central shelter there's a glade of trimmed grass where a boy and a girl are doing yoga, muscles glistening in the sun as they both hold a one-handed posture, legs and bodies hovering parallel to the ground until they tremble and slowly lower themselves.

"Activities at Wildhaven are down to what individuals enjoy and are good at," says Iona. "I've got a few things to do. Would you two like to rest or take a look around?"

We reply at the same moment. I say I wouldn't mind a rest, while Poppy says we'll take a look. We roll our eyes at each other.

"Well. When you feel like going to your hut, just ask anyone, they'll show you."

Iona gives my arm a squeeze. Poppy's eyes widen as she scans around. I slip my hand into my pocket and find my phone.

"I'm sorry, Aster," Iona says. "We have a no-tech policy at Wildhaven—that's the point of the camp. Is it OK if I look after it for you? There's nowhere to charge it anyway."

I frown but pass it over to her.

She turns to Poppy, eyebrows raised.

"Mom wouldn't let me have a phone until I'm twelve," she says.

God, she's such a good liar.

Iona presses her lips together, then forces them into a sad smile. I realize it's the first time we've mentioned Mom and look away as my chest tightens.

"You're free to go anywhere you like within the camp boundary. I'll find you later," says Iona.

She disappears between the huts. I can't figure my aunt out. She has this kind of aura of cheerful calm, yet nothing about her is relaxed. She particularly didn't seem relaxed when she saw that quad bike in the forest. And I didn't know she was involved in anything like this. There was a photo of her on our fridge at home, giving an injection to a small child in a tent in Africa, another grainy newspaper article about a team of doctors who administered chemotherapy in war zones.

But I guess we don't know the real Iona. The whole situation of having to be our guardian might be awkward for her.

Poppy takes out her phone and snaps a photo of the students working at the central hut.

"Don't," I say, glaring at her. No one has noticed.

"What?" she says.

She takes another photo of the yoga pair.

"Poppy," I say in a warning tone. She gives me a fake smile but shoves the phone back in her pocket.

"Let's walk around the outside of the camp," I say.

"Mmm, let's," says Poppy sarcastically, and I widen my eyes at her.

One hut is bigger, older-looking, and stands a little apart from the others. We stop at the door. There's no one around.

"She did say we could go anywhere," says Poppy.

I knock on the door. No answer. I check around, then push it open a crack and crane my neck. It's dim inside. There's a hammock and desk with a laptop open on top, a small yellow sticky note in the corner of the black screen. I remember how Mom loved a sticky note. *Get milk*. That was the last one I remember. Why didn't I keep it? My throat shrinks, hot and narrow.

Poppy holds the door, whispering, "So much for no technology."

"And no electricity," I say, swallowing down the memory and focusing on Poppy.

She takes a photo of the inside of the hut, and this time I lunge for her phone, but she snatches it away.

"There you are." Iona's voice behind us almost makes us jump out of our skin. Poppy stuffs the phone in the front pocket of her hoodie before we spin around.

"Sorry," I say, feeling my cheeks flush.

"It's no problem. My laptop runs on a battery pack I recharge in town. I need it for keeping in contact with a couple of colleagues at the university and for collating the results of the study," she says.

I nod, avoiding eye contact, waiting for her to ask for Poppy's phone. Poppy kicks at the ground with the toe of her boot.

"Come on, a couple of us were about to gather some herbs. Why don't you come along?" says Iona, slipping her arms through each of ours. She didn't see the phone.

Poppy sighs. "Mom loved picking stuff for us to eat. We used to catch a bus to the countryside on Sunday afternoons. She'd make us try flower petals and all sorts of plants. Even nettles. We boiled them, do you remember, Ast? They were gross," she says. I know she's changing the subject to cover up the phone, but she's talking about Mom, so as usual I can't reply. I glance over Poppy's head, across to Iona, and see something in the slowness of her blink that makes me wonder if her grief is like mine, buried and sore, like a festering splinter.

"As you know, our parents also died young, and our mom had cancer. I understand what you are going through," says Iona. I look down at my boots.

There's a pause.

"But you got over it, didn't you?" says Poppy.

A longer pause. "I guess I found ways to live through it."

I brace one hand against the hut, suddenly dizzy with everything that has happened. I feel Iona looking at me, but she doesn't say anything else.

We spend the rest of the afternoon foraging, and I learn how to spot amaranth and burdock, chicory and young plantain leaves, with a tall boy and a girl who smiles a lot. She has dark brown skin and wears her Afro pushed back from her face by a plaited scarf. I hear the boy call her Beti. She sounds like she might be African. The boy has a pale complexion and is tall and serious with short dark hair; his accent could be eastern European, and he introduces himself as Dimi. They must have a lot of foreign students at the university, but it feels rude to ask them where they are from when they don't ask anything about us. For once I wish Poppy would shoot out her usual volley of questions, but even she seems shy around them.

The time passes quickly, and after bowls of stew with seeded bread by the fire, Poppy and I are both yawning, although it's barely even twilight. Iona leads us to a low hut and pushes open the door, and I see our backpacks. Shadows fall into the creases across her forehead and by the sides of her mouth.

"It would be great if you could wear these heart-rate monitors, just at night." She holds out her hand, offering me two black rubber wristbands. "I track the sleep patterns of everyone in camp as part of the study."

I take them from her with a shrug. "OK."

Mom had worn something similar for a while, tracking the number of steps she'd taken in a day; it was always a lot, as she was a nurse. I snap it on my wrist and pass the other to Poppy.

"Sleep in as long as you like tomorrow, you've traveled half the globe," says Iona, then pauses, looking at me. "You can relax now."

I smile and say a stiff, "Good night."

The hut is bare besides two low beds with woolen blankets and rush mats on the floor, lit by a clay lamp. It smells strongly of new timber. Poppy strips off her clothes quicker than I do and pulls on a pair of pink Hello Kitty pajamas. They are far too small for her; she's never been good at new clothes, preferring her old favorites, even when she's grown out of them.

"Let's ask Iona to take us back tomorrow," says Poppy. "Go to the hotel she talked about."

I blink at her in surprise. She's been rolling her eyes at me since we arrived, but she seemed to have accepted Iona.

"Why are you looking at me like that? This place is totally weird," she says. "I mean, where do they all come from, anyway?"

"She told us. Most are international students," I say.

"OK, then. But I think it's strange that none of them have New Zealand accents," says Poppy, planting her hands on her hips, one eyebrow raised, "and I'm surprised *you* want to stay."

Her emphasis on the "you" sparks my irritation. I remind myself Poppy is only eleven and it's been a really long day.

"Let's talk about it in the morning when we aren't so tired," I say, keeping my voice level. I climb into bed. Poppy continues to stand.

"You're OK with her taking your phone and monitoring us when we're sleeping? Because *that's* not creepy at all."

"I didn't want any of this, either." My voice comes out snappier than I mean it to.

"I get it. Iona is our guardian now, so what I think doesn't matter. You don't have to look after me anymore, so that's a relief for you," she says.

I close my eyes. On the rare occasions we argue, it always escalates too quickly.

"She's not our mom, Aster," says Poppy. Her words are a thump to my chest.

I grind my teeth together to stop myself saying anything back because I'm suddenly hot with fury, but my anger isn't at Poppy. She just wants to talk to me about Mom, but I can't and I hate that. I hate it all.

Poppy wriggles under the woolen blankets, pulls them to her chin, and turns away from me. When I hear her sucking her thumb my anger deflates like a burst balloon.

Poppy gave up sucking her thumb when she was seven.

I'm in my bed. Mom's still at home.

"Mommy!"

It's Poppy, her voice panicked and muffled; she sounds too far away.

I spring up, immediately alert. What's happened?

When I push open Mom's bedroom door, I see she's not in bed. The oxygen tube she wears nearly all the time lies abandoned on her crumpled covers, hissing.

"Mom?"

Poppy is sobbing, but I can't find her. I run through the flat, flinging open doors, searching.

Mom and Poppy both gone—

My eyes spring open into the here and now, and reality streams in like the moonlight through the cracks in the hut. Despair drapes over me, a suffocating blanket, and the hiss of Mom's oxygen machine lingers in my ears. My whole body battles the truth with rasping breaths, fingers tingling, heart hammering in my throat.

Poppy turns in her bed, blinks, and springs out to kneel next to me. She brushes a hair from my cheek.

"Ast? Do the breaths. Three in, six out. In through the nose, out through the mouth. Come on, count. In, two, three. Out, two, three, four . . ."

Poppy is mimicking what Mom would say, and I count with her until my breathing slows and I feel nearer to normal. We caught the panic quick enough, before it could develop into a full-blown attack. I'm able to think again, and shame sweeps through me. I should be taking care of my younger sister, not the other way around.

"Sorry, Pops."

Poppy shrugs. She climbs into my bed without asking and turns to the wall. I curve around her, shivering; a panic attack always leaves me cold and hollowed out. I remember that the wristband is monitoring my heart rate and wonder what Iona will make of that little episode. I sigh. But I don't take it off.

"It will be OK," I say.

Poppy doesn't reply.

"Night, Astronomer," she says finally, voice slurred around her thumb.

"Night, Popstar," I say.

Poppy rests her cold feet against my shins, and I don't complain. My face is inches from the back of her neck, and her hair smells like a baby animal. She still has her braids in; I never remind her to brush her hair, and I always forget to check if she's brushed her teeth. I hear her suck her thumb again, and I close my eyes, swept with a desperate fear that something bad will happen to Poppy because I can't look after her properly.

Iona will never be our mom, but I need her.

3

I hadn't expected to get back to sleep but must have fallen deeply. I wake to the sound of voices from outside. For less than a second—less than a tenth of a second—Mom is alive and it was all a bad dream. Then my limbs are made of lead and my heart is forced back into the labored rhythm of living without her.

Dust motes spin in rays of sunlight that stream through cracks in the hut walls. Poppy is not in my bed, and hers is empty. My panic attack in the night comes back to me with a hot sick feeling, and I recall what Poppy said before we fell asleep about wanting to leave. I don't know what to do if she really hates it here. Everything is so exhausting without Mom. Sitting on the side of the low bed, I stretch and wish she'd woken me and we'd gone out there together. I dress quickly and rummage around for my comb but can't find it, so I attempt to scrape my fingers through my curls, give up, and bundle my hair into a loose ponytail. I slip off the heart-rate monitor and leave it on the bed, then head out of the hut, blinking in the sunshine.

"Aster," calls Iona. She's sitting on a long bench, Poppy beside her. Faces turn to look at me but don't linger, and I return a few polite *good mornings*.

"Look, Ast, I'm eating raisins," says Poppy.

It's a joke; Mom once denied she'd put raisins in a curry because Poppy was refusing to eat fruit at the time. Every night when she called us for dinner we would answer, "Is there raisins?" in singsong voices and then collapse into giggles. It doesn't sound that funny now, but at the time it never seemed to get old.

Despite the sharpness of the memory of Mom, I grin at her. "Giant raisins, even," I say, and she grins back. Just like that, Poppy and I are back to being like we always are.

I survey the wooden plates. The giant raisins look like prunes; there are berries and some sort of cured beef. Not my usual choice of breakfast, but my stomach rumbles and I help myself.

Iona runs a hand over her short buzz of hair. "It's our health check today, where I monitor the effects of the Wildhaven lifestyle. I thought you girls should have checkup's along with the others—some simple tests to make sure you are fit and well. OK?"

When Poppy shrugs I give Iona a nod.

After breakfast, Iona leads us outside to the bigger hut where we saw the laptop the day before. The laptop is still there, but now the screen is bright, displaying a spreadsheet of numbers. Next to it is an open medical case with equipment inside. The hut is lighter; windows that must have been shuttered are now open. She directs us to sit on two wooden stools.

The medical check is in-depth. Iona tests our hearing, vision, and the reflexes in our elbows and knees, and then takes our blood pressure, pulse, height, and weight. She spends a long time listening to our chests, then gets us to blow into a tube with a dial on the side, do jumping jacks for a minute, and blow into it again.

"You are both due for tetanus booster injections," she says.

Before I can say anything, she turns and takes a syringe from a tray and taps the top of the needle. Poppy's sleeve is already raised from the blood-pressure monitor. Iona takes her arm.

"Ready?" she says.

Poppy nods and screws her eyes shut, and with a sharp sip of breath, the injection is done.

I frown. "Do we really need—?"

"Everyone needs to be up to date with tetanus vaccinations. You are working with the soil, with tools, and cuts can happen, and medical care isn't as easy to get to as I'd like," Iona says lightly, already preparing a second syringe. She crosses over to me, and this time she doesn't even ask if I'm ready before piercing my upper arm with it. As she depresses the plunger, I watch the half-syringe-full of creamy liquid disappear into my skin with a sharp tingly feeling. I don't flinch at medical stuff anymore; I helped the nurses a lot with Mom's care toward the end.

"All done. You two are in perfect health," says Iona. "Now take a seat outside for a little while in case you feel light-headed."

Poppy and I sit down on the bench outside the hut, and she shuffles close, her hot breath in my ear.

"You have to admit this place is freaky. Did you see how quickly she did those jabs without giving us a chance to argue? Doctors are supposed to explain stuff to kids, we do have rights—"

She stops mid-sentence as a man approaches the door of the hut carrying a heavy-looking silver box. He's white and about Iona's age, with dark hair graying at the temples. Not a student, then. His face is broad across the cheekbones, his eyes bright turquoise-blue.

He starts back, apparently surprised to see us, and then smiles. "Hello. We haven't met, I—"

Before he can finish, Iona appears at the door.

"Jonathan. Come in," she says. Her voice is as tight as the expression on her face. When the man strides past us, the case he's carrying rattles, as though it contains glass.

"If you are feeling OK, girls, you can go now," she says. She doesn't manage a smile as she closes the door behind us.

Poppy and I stand outside, not moving. There are muffled voices from inside, the word "What . . ." then whispers. Poppy grabs my hand and pulls me to the side of the hut. She finds a chink between the planks, cups her hands around her ear, and leans in. I hesitate for a moment before doing the same.

". . . your involvement is no longer needed. All there is to do is wait, and then I will be in touch." Iona's voice is low, reasonable.

"We agreed we would continue to take blood samples. We need to confirm . . ."

". . . Jonathan. When I saw your quad bike, I presumed you'd been collecting your things from the lab. If I find you've been taking further samples—"

"You will what, Iona? What exactly will you do?"

There's silence, and Poppy and I stare at each other. Her lips are turned down, her eyes wide. The man has that formal way of speaking of someone with excellent English, even though it is not his first language.

Iona's voice again. "Show me what is in the case."

"Iona. It really does not need to come to . . ."

There's a tinkle of breaking glass, and the man curses in a language I don't recognize. There's movement inside, away from us, closer to the door. We dart away from the wall and around the back of the hut. Their voices are now outside, angry whispers, and Poppy has her phone out again, leaning around the hut and snapping a photo of them. I drag her back out of sight, wanting to shake her, and hold my breath, waiting for Iona to discover we've been eavesdropping. We wait until they are gone.

"What do you think that was all about?" says Poppy.

"Don't know. I guess we should ask Iona," I say.

We stroll back to the front of the hut, trying to look normal, and spot the man striding into the trees on the other side of the grassy area that surrounds Wildhaven. No sign of Iona, and the door to her hut is ajar. Poppy raises her eyebrows at me, and I push it open. There's a wet patch on the dirt floor and a glint of broken glass. I step closer, the back of my neck tingling. Poppy stands watch at the door as I crouch and touch the spillage. My finger is stained dark red. That man had something glass in his case containing blood? I shudder and wipe my finger on the inside of my T-shirt before Poppy can see.

"What was it?"

I shrug. "Just broken glass."

I don't want to scare her.

As we start back toward the main hut, Iona walks toward us, a bundle of fishing rods slung over her shoulder.

"Thought you might help us catch some supper?" she says. We follow her across the field around the huts, toward the trees. Poppy nudges me.

"Was that the guy who owned the quad bike?" I ask Iona.

"Jonathan? Yes. He's gone now. If you see him again, tell me right away."

"Have you had an argument with him?" says Poppy, and her innocent voice isn't exactly convincing.

Iona turns to both of us. "A disagreement. His contract is over now. He's a doctor, and he was analyzing samples to monitor the lifestyle effects of Wildhaven, but we don't need him anymore. He has had a little trouble accepting that."

Poppy and I say nothing. I'm not sure what to make of what we just saw.

"If you carry on along this path, you'll find some others at the cliffs, they'll show you the way down. I'll catch up with you."

Iona hands us the fishing rods and strides back across the meadow.

Poppy glares at me. "You've got to admit she is weird," she whispers.

We meet three of the students—Beti and Dimi and another girl—at the clifftop and scramble down to spend the rest of the day in a rocky cove with a stretch of grayish gritty sand. The coastline here wouldn't be in a tourist brochure, but it's good to be at the beach. Iona brings a packed lunch of folded flatbreads and cold mushrooms cooked in garlic, which tastes much better than it looks. Neither of us hooks a fish, but it's a nice way to spend time. Nearly the whole camp arrives over the course of the afternoon; some work on weaving lobster cages out of slim branches of wood, and others attempt to harpoon fish with homemade spears. On the rocks, I watch a girl pull up a series of netlike structures, and Beti explains they are oyster nurseries. The sun is warm, and a couple of the students strip to their underwear, unembarrassed, and swim. I imagine the feel of the clear water surrounding and holding me. I consider taking off my shoes, dabbling my feet, but grief closes its fist around my throat. I can't. I haven't swum, not since Mom.

Midafternoon Poppy complains of a headache. It isn't like her to ever be ill, and it gives me an anxious feeling, a throwback from when Mom was on chemotherapy and the treatment suppressed her immune system, so even one of us having a cold was dangerous. When I feel Poppy's forehead, she's really warm. I call Iona over.

"The tetanus jab can affect some people like this," she says. "I'm going to take you both back to the hut for a lie-down."

We follow her across the clearing, and I'm surprised when Poppy takes my hand. She really *must* be feeling bad. Her fingers close tight, hot and dry around mine, and the sun seems very bright, hurting the backs of my eyes. I'm relieved to see the cluster of huts—I'm not feeling so great myself.

By the time Poppy and I collapse onto our beds, we are both groaning. The fever is accompanied by powerful aches in our joints and blaring headaches behind the eyes. I shiver so much my teeth chatter, yet I'm burning hot. I'm so worried about Poppy. I want my mom.

When Iona lays a cloth on my head, I hold her wrist, her skin cold against mine.

"You'll both be fine," she whispers. "It's just a fever and will break soon."

The next time I wake I feel completely different. Hollow and shaky, but not feverish or in pain. Iona isn't there, and Poppy is curled on her side, still asleep. I stagger across to her and lay the back of my hand on her forehead. Her skin has cooled, and I close my eyes and slump out a breath in relief. The black heart-rate monitor band is on her wrist, and mine is in place too, but I definitely didn't put it on—I was feeling far too ill. Iona must have done it. There are noises outside. The light is golden, like sunrise. I sit on the edge of the bed, wobbly but better.

4

Poppy sleeps until almost lunchtime, then we get up and wander through camp, vaguely looking for Iona. I'm beginning to recognize the faces of the students and remember some of their names, but they don't introduce themselves. It's like they've been told not to, and it's starting to feel a bit strange when they almost act like they can't see us, although they are friendly enough if we ask a question. Their activities are interesting: boat building, rope making, fishing, cooking, and foraging.

Iona is nowhere to be seen, so we join in the activities when someone looks up and gestures us over. Poppy and I don't need to stick together, but we do. Poppy seems to be accepting this place more, but I keep thinking about the man, Dr. Jonathan, and the argument between him and Iona. I'm beginning to feel like we are in a giant containment pen, like a safari park enclosure. I can't imagine being here for more than a couple of weeks.

It's almost like Iona reads my mind, because that evening around the fire, she suggests a dawn boat trip to a ring of islands a couple of hours offshore.

"There are some rare bioluminescent algae in bloom. It's quite a sight, sets the whole sea aglow, violet. What do you think?"

The students respond enthusiastically, grinning and asking questions, and Poppy and I nod, a bit surprised and very exhausted.

Iona wakes us just before sunrise.

She lays a pile of material on the end of my bed. "We'll be snorkeling, so you'll need to wear these," she says.

She leaves, and Poppy and I stare at each other, bleary-eyed. I unfold the clothing she's left us. There is a swimsuit each in silvery gray, then another suit for each of us in the same material with long sleeves and legs and a black zip up the front. It even has a hood. I give it a dubious look.

"I'm definitely wearing my hoodie over the top."

Poppy nods. "Do you want to go? We don't have to."

I pause, meeting her eyes through a slice of moonlight across the dark hut. "Well, the bioluminescent stuff does sound cool," I say.

"Yeah, I guess," says Poppy. We give each other tentative smiles. Poppy is right, this place is definitely not normal. And I'm not sure I want to snorkel, if I'm even ready to swim yet.

Outside the huts, the others are already gathered, dressed the same as we are, some wearing sweatshirts or T-shirts over the gray suits. I am surprised when Iona heads to the back of the group and a tall boy named Darnell with deep-brown skin takes the lead at a swift pace so we almost have to jog. I wonder what the hurry is as Darnell leads us along the cliff path, past the beach we were on the day before.

Then Iona appears back in front, directing us to where a dip in the cliff meets the rocks from the beach below and we can scramble down. The bay is different from the one we were on yesterday: small, with coarse, gravelly grayish sand and pebbles, secluded from the rest of the coastline. A rowing boat rests onshore, and a little way out a larger boat is anchored, the size of the ferries we took between islands when we went on vacation to Greece.

Poppy stuffs her phone into her pocket and as everyone follows Iona down the beach, she drops back and leaves her hoodie bundled behind a rock. I see her checking whether it is visible from the cliff. What is she playing at now? I glare at her, but I recognize the stubborn look she shoots back at me, so I say nothing. Let's just hope the phone is still there when we get back.

We cram into the rowing boat, and I read the name painted in bold italics at the back. *Deep Retreat*. I count nineteen of us including Iona.

At last Poppy and I climb the rungs at the back of the second boat. It's bigger than it looked, and the back deck is dominated by what seems to be a beige-colored shipping container made of corrugated metal, the size of one of those small offices you see on building sites.

"Hey—look!" The boy behind me points back toward the forest. Plumes of smoke rise in the distance, dark against the mid-blue dawn sky.

Everyone turns. The underside of the smoke cloud glows orange; even at this distance I see bursts of tiny sparks above the tree canopy. Poppy grips my arm.

"Oh, it will just be a small forest fire, they produce so much smoke," says Iona. "It's north of Wildhaven, nothing to worry about. Remember we have a firebreak all around the camp." She seems a little out of breath. Her eyes are steady, but beads of sweat glisten at her temples as she ushers us all into the cabin. I turn. Beti is hanging back, chewing her lip as she stares back at the fire, but when another girl links arms with her, she smiles and lets her friend pull her into the cabin.

Iona closes the door behind her. She switches on the lights, and everything seems better. When the others start to chat, my shoulders drop and my heart settles into a regular beat. The cabin is a long room with windows on three sides and sets of dining tables and chairs at the front. The rows of soft recliners at the back provide more than enough space for all of us to sit down, and Poppy and I take two seats near the door.

Iona closes a window, although the cabin is stale-smelling and warm. The boat rocks, and I feel queasy.

"The journey won't be too long," says Iona. "We're heading to a beautiful group of islands where the algae only blooms once every few years, it's going to be a real treat to see it. We are perfectly safe."

"It's stuffy in here," says Poppy, her voice almost drowned out by the rising noise of the engine.

Iona's words stutter in my mind. *Perfectly safe.* Why wouldn't we be?

A hissing sound. I scan around for its source.

A rush of air hits my legs at the same time as a metallic tang stings my nostrils. I frown. Vibrations travel through my seat, jangling my teeth as the engine revs. I look around for the source of the smell and find a thin jet of steam shooting from a box on the floor at my feet. But it isn't steam. It isn't hot. It's like the dry ice in chemistry at school.

I stand. Iona is now sitting, clasping a white mask over her nose and lips.

What? What is she *doing*? My heart races, and I go from confusion to panic in a flash.

I clap my hand over my mouth and turn to Poppy, grabbing her hand and shoving it to her face, shaking my head. *Don't breathe in*. We need to get out. Now.

I grasp Poppy's free hand and pull her along the row of seats. There's a girl in front of us—we've worked with her once on rope making, and I recognize her unusual long red hair. Sunee. She holds my fingers tight and mouths something that looks like, "It's OK." Snatching my hand back, I freeze as the girl's chest rises and she draws a deep breath of the mist through her nose. I stare, fascinated, horrified, as her eyes roll back. Her head lolls sideways toward me.

Vapor now pours from what must be more of the black boxes, dispersing throughout the cabin.

Iona is wearing a *gas mask*.

This is no snorkeling trip.

We scramble over Sunee—unconscious? Worse?—and another boy who is sprawled on the floor. Mist billows into clouds; the hiss competes with gasps, muffled screams, and the rising engine noise. The sounds suggest not everyone is taking this as calmly as Sunee, but I can't see anyone now—the fog is too thick. Moisture clings to my skin.

Staggering to the door, I drag Poppy, my lungs now burning for breath. A boy is curled at the base of the door. Dead? I can't think about that. I twist the handle, back and forth, back and forth. Locked. I bang the window beside it with my fist.

Panic courses through my veins. I can't hold my breath for much longer and need to find something to shatter the glass. There's nothing. I crash my fist against the glass again and again.

Poppy is a hazy outline in the mist, then she drops my hand and her fists are next to mine, pounding on the glass.

My thoughts spool out, one flowing into the next, trying to find something that makes sense, something that will help us.

Thud.

Fists sliding across the glass, now slick with condensation. Why would Iona do this? The fences, the secrecy . . .

Thud.

No one knows we were at Wildhaven. No one. Sam from the plane. No—he only had a road sign to go by and no reason to ever think of us again. Iona organized this so that what she's doing will never be discovered.

The fire. It was the camp. Deliberate.

But she's Mom's *sister.*

Poppy's fists drop. I grab her by the shoulders as her mouth opens and our eyes search each other's, frantic, as if the answer can be found in the space connected by our gaze.

Poppy sensed something was wrong here; why didn't I listen?

My sister slumps forward into my arms, and I collapse to my knees with the weight of her. *Dead weight.* No. I'll resuscitate her, we'll get free, jump overboard . . .

Sparks of light flicker across my vision. She's slipping from my grip, too heavy.

Poppy!

My chest burns with desperation and I gasp.

Cold in my mouth.

A sour plastic tang on my tongue.

Wetness in my lungs.

It doesn't hurt. Poppy isn't in pain. The fog penetrates my mind, lifting me free from myself. I can't feel my body at all.

Everything is bleached whiter and whiter. Images flash by: Poppy on a swing, Mom at the side of the pool.

Reach.

Kick.

Breathe.

Mom with Iona, spilling red wine on the carpet. Laughing. The name on the side of the boat.

Deep. Retreat.

I lose sense of where I am. What I am. There is only . . . nothing.

Shiny. A cloud. Way way up.

It can't hold us. We'll fall.

White.

Gray.

Black.

Safe.

Perfectly . . . safe.

5

Sam wakes to the chug and hiss of the coffee machine downstairs, swings into a sitting position on the edge of the bed, and rubs his face. It's his first day off from his summer job since he got back from Auckland, and he's planning to ride out to have a look for the ecovillage the girls on the plane talked about. No one he's asked seemed to know anything about it, and the photo Poppy sent made him curious. He starts to thump down the stairs two at a time, then stops himself, padding the remaining steps on the balls of his feet as he remembers Granda might still be asleep if he's feeling poorly.

Mom is an architect and often works from home. She's already hunched at her desk in the corner drawing lines on her sloped trackpad, which then appear across one of the two huge monitors in front of her.

"Hey, you're up early," she says, only turning briefly to shoot Sam a distracted smile.

"You too," says Sam.

"I'm on a deadline. I'll be done in a couple of hours, then I'm taking Granda to the clinic," says Mom.

"For the treatment trial?" says Sam.

"No—a scan." Mom nods, but he can see the worry around her eyes. "His oncologist has seen real shrinkage in the tumor, and if it continues it might become operable. Granda says it's due to this trial; I'd like a few more details about it, but he's signed some disclaimer."

Sam's relief makes him feel lighter. He didn't dare ask how it was going when he arrived back from Auckland a week ago. But Granda is getting better, of course he is, he's strong. Mom turns back to her work.

"Granda's in the kitchen now, so breakfast is probably the full works. Please eat my share and his if you can manage it. He's driving me mad."

Sam grins as his tummy rumbles.

Granda kicks open the kitchen door, a wooden tray in one hand, coffeepot in the other, accompanied by the smell of sausages. He's a tall, broad-shouldered man, young for a granddad, fifty-nine last birthday. His springy curls are growing back and look like a fluffy gray halo. Sam feels a surge of affection accompanied by that hollow feeling in his stomach. He remembers the girls on the plane and can't imagine not having Granda anymore.

"Made your favorite today, chook," Granda booms at Sam's mom, treating Sam to one of his stage winks. She tuts.

"I hope you're not eating all this, Dad? Remember your cholesterol, the doctors say light foods—"

"If cancer can't finish me, I'm hardly going to be knocked off by a sausage or three." Granda catches the expression on Mom's face and sets the tray on the table. "Don't you fret. I've had rabbit food and juice like an angel. Sam will have no trouble putting this lot away, will you, Sammy?"

"Thanks, Granda. I'm going out on the bike today." Sam pauses. "Over the trails by Mount Hikurangi. See if I can find out what this ecovillage place is about."

Mom turns, leaning on the back of her desk chair, and does the face where her nostrils flare and her eyebrows fly upward. "You still rattling on about the mysterious British girls from the plane?"

Granda wiggles his eyebrows.

Sam is irritated to feel his cheeks flush. The younger sister, Poppy, was funny, and he enjoyed chatting with her. And yeah, OK, the older girl was cute with her corkscrew curly hair the same color as the scrubbed oak floorboards beneath Sam's bare feet and freckles scattered across her skin. Her eyes had danced with fun for a moment as she glared at her sister, but mainly she'd looked a bit—lost.

"Take the spares kit and a pump, food and water, and waterproofs. Keep to the tracks," says Mom, turning back to her desk.

Granda is uncharacteristically quiet. He and Sam used to ride a lot together, but Granda's not ready for even a gentle ride, not yet.

Sam wolfs down some cereal while Granda packs the sausages and hash browns into a plastic box. Sam throws the extra supplies into his bike bag. He's itching to get on his bike, but something makes him grab a quick shower first, even though the odds are he won't find the girls anyhow. He probably won't see anyone at all, not out there.

Sam rides the bus to the sign for Tokomaru Bay and then gets off to follow the trail just before it. After three hours of hard riding, rain clouds are building, the air humid. There's been no sign of any ecovillage or camp. The forest is dense here, mostly untouched. If the camp is small, he hasn't a hope of finding it, but he's intrigued and decides to aim for a view over the tree-tops, so he slogs uphill and stops at a break in the trees to swig some water. High enough. From here he has a clear view to the coast.

Something catches his eye. A fug of smoke hanging above the trees. It's a strangely still day with barely a breath of breeze. Forest fires are not common around here, and it rained yesterday. He narrows his eyes, wishing he had binoculars. The fire seems to be out, just the smoke cloud remains, trapped in the valley. He springs back on his bike and pedals in top gear downhill, then careers along a narrow forest track in the direction of the smoke.

Sam walks his bike through the trees and stops as the sharp scent of woodsmoke fills his nostrils. His heart is steady but seems louder than normal. The ground is black and bald, thick with ash. He whistles through his teeth. That was some fire. It has gouged out a huge circle in this dense forest.

He props his bike against a tree. The scorched ground is covered in a thick layer of charred wood, and he roots through the charcoal with the toes of his shoes as he crunches his way across the circle, looking for anything that hasn't burned, any sign there was anything here but forest. Something glints, and he crouches to pick it up. A piece of broken glass in a bowl shape, around the size of a ten-cent coin. He searches around for other fragments but can't find any. He slips the glass into his jacket pocket and zips it up.

Could this have been the site of the camp the girl was talking about?

Goose bumps rise along his arms. People were definitely here. And something went seriously wrong.

A movement at the other side of the burnt area. A man appears from the trees. He's wearing dark jeans, hiking boots, and a faded cap pulled low, and he carries a backpack on one shoulder and a black plastic bag in his hand. He's raking through the ashes just like Sam had been a few moments ago. With his eyes intent on the ground, he doesn't see Sam.

Sam calls out, "Hey there, do you know what happened here?"

The man's expression of concentration freezes for a second, then breaks into a smile. "Hello!" he calls cheerily. His accent is clipped; European but not British.

Sam scans the man up and down. "Are you with the police?"

The man shakes his head. "No. I saw the smoke. The police were just leaving when I arrived."

"I was out riding," says Sam. "I was looking for an ecovillage."

"An ecovillage? Here?" says the man, titling his head to one side. His eyes are light blue green, and his eyebrows tilt up in the center, giving him an open expression. He seems friendly enough.

"Maybe there wasn't one," says Sam, "just I heard there might be."

"Oh—where did you hear that?" The man waits until Sam feels it would be rude not to answer.

"Just these two British girls I got chatting to, they were on their way to it."

The man nods and lowers his shoulders a fraction, almost like he's satisfied with that answer. "Well, it's a probably a bit remote here for anything like that. Also easy to get lost, but if you follow the coastal path you'll reach Tokomaru Bay."

"Thanks," says Sam, although he hadn't said he was lost. "Hope no one was hurt in the fire?"

"The police said nothing to suggest that, thank heavens," says the man.

They appraise each other for a few more seconds, and the smile on the older guy's face starts to seem a bit fixed.

"Well, I'd better shoot. Looks like rain," says Sam.

The man tips his cap at Sam and walks back into the trees. Sam starts along the track to the beach but hears the faint sound of an engine and stops to listen, frowning. The guy must have come by motorbike or quad, but those aren't allowed in the national park.

Sam turns and rides in what he thinks is the direction of the engine sound until he can no longer hear it. The trail he's following is wider than the usual tracks through this part of the forest, fresh-cut branches showing it is maintained. It leads to a low, square concrete building almost concealed by trees. He circles the outer fence, noting the CCTV cameras mounted at regular intervals. The building is windowless and has the look of a bunker. Some sort of Ministry of Defence place, maybe?

There's not a lot more to see, and Sam cycles back toward the coast. It's a relief when he leaves the forest and stares out across the ocean. Still, gray, no surf today and not a boat in sight. The sky is low, and the air thick—he's going to get drenched. As he wheels along the path, he scans the beaches below, hoping to spot a secret surf break he could come to with his mates another time, but all he sees are rocky coves, too dangerous and tricky to get down to. One looks promising, easy to scramble down the rocks to the sand. He brakes to take a closer look.

There's something there, behind a rock. Clothing?

He checks there's no one around and leaves his bike at the edge of the cliff, then skips down the boulders. The gravelly sand is disturbed; could be footprints, if so—lots of them. A group of people stood in one place, then went down to the sea.

The first fat drop of rain lands on his arm. He grabs the clothing. It's a hoodie: small, purple, with a white zip. He stares.

The girl on the plane was wearing a hoodie just like this.

Poppy.

Sam stares around as the rain patters down. A cold feeling creeps over him. She was definitely wearing one like it; he remembers her sister telling her to stop fiddling with the zip. It can't be a coincidence. He feels the unusual weight of it and slips his hand in the front pocket. It's her phone. Rainbow swirl on the case, he recognizes it for sure. She was here and she left her phone, or her sister's phone. He frowns at the black screen, not quite able to believe what he's found. When he presses the button on the side a dot-pattern passcode request appears and the battery icon flashes only 7 percent charge. He turns it off again.

Sam zips the phone and the hoodie into his bag and pulls on his waterproof jacket. He remembers the charred ground in the forest: silent, black, dead. Was the fire something to do with those girls, their camp? Back up on the coastal path he sees the rain is already clearing the smoke that hung above the fire site. He turns to look over the beach once more. Raindrops thud into the sand, obliterating the footprints.

Later in his room, Sam takes out the girl's phone. It feels wrong to try to unlock it, but maybe it can tell him where they are and he can return it to them. He swipes the black screen—only 6 percent battery now, but it takes the same charger as his and he plugs it in. Sam tries a few shapes on the passcode screen. P for Poppy. A for Aster. C, L, then a square. Nothing. Now he's tried the wrong code too many times and text appears asking for an email address. He curses. He searches the internet for a way to unlock a phone of this make and discovers he's permanently locked it and a factory reset would wipe her photos, contacts, apps, and any data.

Sam slips the phone into a padded envelope to mail to the police station with a note explaining where he found it and his address.

He takes out the glass fragment he found in the ashes and looks at it under his desk lamp. It's familiar, somehow. It doesn't look like part of a bottle; the glass is too thin. A smooth regular bowl shape: small, delicate. It's blackened on the outside, but inside it is dark brown and flaky. He stares at it for a little longer, suddenly reluctant to touch it, then wraps it in a tissue and puts it in the back of his desk drawer.

PART TWO

ADRIFT

NOW

6

"Poppy!" My throat is raw, my voice hoarse. Eyes throbbing in the brightness, I shield my face as my mind judders, searching for memories.

Hand sliding on the door handle. The mist cold in my chest.

My arms were locked tight around her; I would never have let her go, so she must be here.

I pull myself into a kneeling position and ease my hand away from my eyes, narrowing them to slits.

This isn't the same beach we set off from. The sand is softer, pristine, the colors too vivid. There's a turquoise lagoon in front of me, empty. I remember now, we were on a boat, a snorkeling trip. It was dawn . . .

I blink in the dazzling sunlight, call out for Poppy again, and then break off into a coughing fit, rolling back on my side, cheek against the sand. Where is she?

The horizon tilts. Maybe I'm hurt; maybe the boat sank and we've been washed ashore. I can't focus my eyes at any distance, and the air is pressing down on me.

Oh God. Poppy.

I need to calm down, make my mind work.

Black seeps into the edges of my vision. I focus on what floats to the top of my mind, ignoring the deeper layers still clouded. Finding Poppy is all that matters.

I push myself shakily into a sitting position. I'm wearing a gray suit, and I remember Iona gave them to us before we left. I raise my hand to my face, turning it back and forth. Skintight gloves in the same material.

I pat up toward my head. The hood is up, clinging tight; I hook my fingers under an edge and pull it back.

Another figure in the same bodysuit staggers toward me.

Is it her?

I attempt to stand, but my muscles turn to jelly, aching, and I crumple back to the sand. What is *wrong* with me? I grind my teeth together and crawl, arms and shoulders trembling, burning with the effort. So thirsty, my mouth sticky, my tongue thick and swollen.

Liquid dislodges from my ears, and sounds boom, the sea swishing against the sand.

I'm too weak. Black blotches scud across my line of sight.

A thud of feet on the sand.

"Hey, it's OK, drink this," says a voice. I don't dare to look up; I'm close to passing out.

I slurp from something held to my lips. The sweet liquid is like pure relief. Coconut.

"Drink it all, you'll feel better," says the voice. A boy or man with a lilting accent.

I gulp down the last of it and the shakes subside. My mind sharpens.

The boy peers down at me through brown eyes. His red-brown hair is damp and curly, his white skin is scattered with gingery freckles and some acne pockmarks, and he is heavily muscled beneath his gray suit. He looks familiar from camp, and I remember he was one of the students splashing around in the sea when we were fishing.

"You hurt?"

I shake my head. *Poppy.*

I scan over the boy for signs of injury, signs that he's been in an accident.

"I don't think so. My sister. Poppy. Has there . . . ?" I rasp, my voice gravelly. "Where's the boat?"

The boy blinks at me and shakes his head. "I don't know. I thought I was alone, then you just washed up. I'm Callum."

I survey the sea again, trying to force my muddled brain to make sense of this. I *washed* up.

"I remember you. Iona's niece."

"Yes. I need to find my sister. Where is . . . everybody? What do you mean, washed up?"

"I'm not sure. I was so shaky and close to blacking out. I opened a coconut, trying to do something, calm down, and then you were just there on the shore."

He can't be right. None of this can be right. We were on the boat, so where is it now? Callum shakes his head as if he can read my mind and agrees with me. Then he surveys his hands, peeling off the gloves and examining them in confusion. I look down at my own hands, and when I turn them over, I find a bump in the material about an inch above the cuff of the suit. I draw back the clinging material of my sleeve and gasp. A black tube snakes out of the inside of my wrist, just below my hand. I follow the tube beneath the suit material, up my arm, across the inside of my elbow, past my armpit, and over my shoulder. Callum's mouth hangs open as he watches me, then does the same. I feel the tube exit through a hole in the back of the suit.

I realize it's connected to the black sleeveless jacket that snugly encases my torso.

I stare, horrified, at my wrist, where the tube disappears into me. The snorkeling trip was a trick. Iona wanted to get us on board the boat. The fire. She burned the camp.

"What is going on?" I say.

Something has been *done* to me. To *us*.

There was gas on the boat, coming from the black boxes. Iona *gassed* us.

A transparent tube snakes out of my other wrist. Some sort of IV in each arm, rigged up to a black life jacket.

Callum's eyes track past me, and he staggers to his feet, pointing to the lagoon in front of us.

Another body, floating.

I skid down the sand and trip into the water, sending up sheets of spray. The figure travels across the surface of the water toward the beach, but his or her arms and legs don't seem to be moving. Impossible.

I wade out and grab the body. Not Poppy. A girl whose deep-brown skin contrasts with the pale gray hood of the suit. I recognize her as Beti, the girl who took us foraging. I grip her under the armpits and tow her across the surface of the water; she's kept afloat by the same black life vest I'm still wearing. Even though it's mainly Callum who drags her up the sand, my arms tremble with the effort. Her lips are a deep-plum color, bluish around the edges. I crouch at Beti's side as Callum peels transparent tape from her eyelids. There isn't even a flicker of movement in her eyelashes. He leans forward, his ear to her mouth.

"I can't hear her breathing."

My eyes skitter over the beach. If Beti came out of the lagoon and she's—she can't be—then Poppy . . .

Callum's voice breaks into my thoughts. "Aster? She hasn't got a pulse."

I stare at Callum blankly. "I have to go in—my sister."

Callum's voice cracks. "Please—do you know how to help her? Iona showed us, but I can't remember." His eyes shine as they meet mine, desperate, and I recognize the blankness in his face that comes with panic. Suddenly I remember a first aid class at school. An afternoon out of class, all of year nine in the school gym.

I pinch Beti's wrist. I can't feel anything, and I swallow. What now?

More memories from that first aid lesson sweep through my head; there was that dummy torso thing. Check airway, then chest compressions? Isn't there supposed to be a rescue breath first? What *is* a rescue breath?

"She hasn't breathed once, I'm sure. Like—that must be,

what? Nearly a minute. That's bad, isn't it? How many minutes before she . . ." Callum's voice rises.

"You hold her wrist, keep checking for a pulse," I say, forcing a calm voice.

Visions of Poppy flash through my mind. I have to try to help this girl. I collapse into the sand beside Beti's head. Tilt the chin, check the mouth for obstructions. I press my hand against Beti's forehead and take a deep breath, preparing to cover her lips like we did on the plastic dummy thing.

"I felt something!" says Callum. "A pulse in her wrist, I felt it, and she twitched, she's alive!"

I grip Beti's other wrist. Nothing. I wait, and the sea makes a steady rushing sound as if counting for me. Too long. Then a weak throb, followed by another, then nothing again. I adjust my fingers. Another pulse.

"Did you feel it?" says Callum. I nod, and he closes his eyes for a moment in relief.

"It's really slow—I'll try breathing," I say. I tilt her chin and cover her lips with mine. Her skin feels rubbery and yielding, and I shudder; this is nothing like the dummy torsos we practiced on. I breathe hard into her, but the air pushes back into my own mouth, puffing out my cheeks as well as hers. I try again.

"I can't, I'm not doing it right," I say, my whole body trembling.

"But her pulse is better, here, feel," says Callum. He's right. It's still slow, but at least it is steady, a beat every few seconds.

A hiss fills my ears. I'm panting. Callum looks up and meets my eyes for a moment.

Not now.

The panic can't rise *now.* I focus in on the details around me, the sound of the sea lapping, the sand crunching beneath my knees. *Three breaths in, six breaths out.*

Callum holds Beti's wrist and says something else, but I'm tuned out; everything seems to stop as we wait, my eyes combing the sea. Maybe it doesn't matter now if Beti has a pulse. If she's not breathing, she'll die from lack of oxygen. It's already been too long.

This is a nightmare. It has to be. Just a nightmare, so I'm going to wake up.

I lean closer to check her breathing again, then her body gives a tiny shudder, and I think I've imagined it, but when Callum's eyes dart up to meet mine I know he felt it too. Before he can say anything, Beti's chest heaves, and Callum releases his hold as thick liquid gushes from her lips, milky and blue. Arm under her head, he lifts her so she's tipped to the side. At the same time as relief floods me, I shift back, horrified at what I'm seeing. What is that *stuff* she's spewing up? It certainly isn't seawater, and it's coming from her lungs. Her eyes are still closed, her body limp.

I'm about to suggest we lay her in the recovery position when she splutters, arms flinging up and around Callum's neck as she wakes up, spitting the last of the bluish gloop down his back.

"Is she OK, is she breathing?" says Callum.

I nod. She's coughing, so she must have air in her lungs. Coughing is a sign the body is well enough to protect itself, getting rid of what it doesn't need. When things are really bad, there's no coughing. I learned that from Mom.

Beti is now flopped over Callum's shoulder; her lips look a better color, and her eyelids flutter as she gasps in breaths. I glance across the lagoon. We don't know she's OK. She went far too long without breathing.

Even though I'm disgusted, I touch a blob of the bluish liquid resting on the sand before it soaks in. It's warm and slippery between my finger and thumb and reminds me of laundry liquid. I gingerly sniff it. It smells faintly synthetic. Medical. This is the same stuff I was coughing up, I remember now.

"What *is* it?" says Callum, still gripping Beti tight.

I shrug and notice that one tear has spilled over and wet his cheek. His face shivers with relief; I don't know how to tell him that this is not all right, that his friend had too little oxygen for far too long.

Beti leans back, her arms still around Callum's neck, eyes unfocused. "Wha goin on?" she says in a slurred voice.

My eyes blink rapidly in disbelief.

"Hello, Beti, you just vommed down my back. No need to apologize," says Callum, his voice gruff. He sniffs, looking down at her with a trembling smile.

Beti lifts her head, blinks, and coughs again, detaching herself from Callum. "Oh, it's only you, Cal. What's wrong?"

Callum laughs, and then his face crumples and he presses it against Beti's shoulder. He reaches a hand over to me, and although I don't know this boy at all, I grip his fingers very tight in shared relief.

I stand. The lagoon is glassy, enclosed by a rocky reef. Behind it, the sun catches on the whitecaps of small waves. A fringe of palms lines the pale golden beach behind us. The sun is hot, too hot. Tropical. This is nothing like the beach we were on—it doesn't even look like New Zealand. I need to find Poppy.

What I just saw was impossible. Beti's heart was too slow, and she went too long without oxygen. I've heard of people falling through ice and surviving when they had been declared dead, but there is no ice here—far from it.

Beti sits on the sand, shading her eyes, and Callum blows out a long ragged breath, wiping his cheeks with his fist.

"We thought you were dead," he says. "You weren't breathing for ages."

Beti is still disoriented, and Callum fetches another coconut and helps her sip.

"I need to go out there, in the lagoon, and look for the others," I say.

"I don't get this, but I don't think the boat sank," says Callum. "We're not injured and—"

"This must be the next one," finishes Beti.

Callum glares at her, and his eyes dart to me, but she shrugs, indicating the lagoon in front of us.

"What? She's going to find out now, isn't she?" she says.

My eyes flick from Beti to Callum. "What are you talking about?"

"The way we got here—seriously messed up," says Callum, "but this must be what Iona was training us for. The next Wildhaven."

7

“How can this be the *next* Wildhaven?” I say, my voice trembling with frustration. The life vest pulls at my shoulders, constricts my chest. I unzip it, then remember I’m rigged up to it by the tubes at my wrists. I need to get into that lagoon and look for Poppy.

Callum surveys the tubes in his wrists with a frown, and I see he genuinely isn’t any more familiar with this bizarre outfit than I am.

"Need to get free of this," I say.

I yank on the left tube with my eyes screwed tight, and then it's free—revealing a narrower tube that must have been in my vein, stained pink with blood. I feel sick.

Callum and Beti exchange looks, but neither says anything. We stand at the edge of the lagoon, the teal-blue water smooth, unbroken.

"So you guys were expecting to be here? But not like this?" My voice comes out through gritted teeth as I yank the other tube from my right wrist with a sharp scratch and hold it up.

Both Callum and Beti look horrified, then he squares his shoulders and tries to sound nonchalant.

"We knew one day we'd be relocated somewhere more remote. We had survival training for tropical areas," says Callum.

"But not like this. The snorkeling trip was a ruse, but why didn't Iona just tell us? And rigging us up with tubes and coughing up blue stuff? It makes no sense," says Beti. "Sorry, Aster. Iona said there would be a right time and place to tell you properly about Wildhaven, just not right away."

I rein in my questions and focus on drilling them for only the information I need right now. I shrug off the jacket, letting it drop to the sand.

"So where are the others? Why aren't they here?" I feel desperate.

Beti bends and picks up a couple of pieces of driftwood.

"We need to get a fire started," she says.

A fire? They want to make *camp*? My panic overrides reasonable thought. It's impossible that Poppy isn't here. She was in my arms, and I would never have let her go, no matter what. Without thinking I cup my mouth and yell, "Poppy!"

My call echoes across the lagoon and returns to me as if it has nothing to report.

I hold my throat. I'm at what the therapist would call a "high level of background anxiety," my thought processes erratic and muddled, panic close. I blow out a long, slow breath. I'm supposed to acknowledge the anxious feelings and let them pass on by, ground myself in the here and now. I look down at my wrists. There are twin beads of blood at the holes the tubes left.

"I'm going to search the lagoon." I'm managing to sound calm. That's good.

"I'll come with you," says Callum.

I glance at him. His hair flops forward, drying into reddish waves. He's a few inches taller than I am and his muscles bulge, but bulky boys aren't usually the best in the water.

"Are you a good swimmer?" I say.

He gives a half nod, half shrug. "Iona liked us to swim, and I used to fish with my dad. He made me swim laps around the boat, no matter how rough or cold it was, to make sure I wouldn't freak out if I fell in."

When I meet his eyes, he looks away and swings his arms as

though limbering up. I realize he's trying to put on the brave face he didn't have earlier, embarrassed now by his reaction when we were reviving Beti.

"OK, then. We need goggles," I say.

Beti points to a wide equipment pouch strapped to my waist. I hadn't even noticed it beneath the life vest. I locate a pair of minimalist-looking goggles inside. There's other stuff in there, but I zip it back up and put on the goggles.

I wade into the water.

Callum snaps his goggles in place. We are both still in our gray bodysuits.

Beti has already collected a neat pile of driftwood. "I want to come with you, but someone should stay. In case," she says.

Callum squeezes her arm. "We won't leave the lagoon," he says, and the way his eyes cling to her face tells me he still can't believe she's OK.

I pause for a moment.

I have to do this for Poppy.

Mom's voice.

Reach. Kick. Bre—

I shut down her voice in my head. Not now.

Inhaling deeply, I plunge into the lagoon as if it is cold and will take my breath, but the water is surprisingly warm. My legs and arms remember what to do, and the water calms me like it always has even though it's been months since I was in the pool.

I adjust the goggles and survey the pale seabed through clear water. The lagoon is at least five times the size of a swimming pool and slopes gradually away from the beach, leveling out at around three or four meters deep. The reef that protects it protrudes from the water in a broken line, almost completely encircling the turquoise water within.

I skim along the surface, Callum close by. My eyes reach across the seabed, and my heart curls tight in my chest with fear of what I might find, but the rippled sand of the lagoon bottom is empty of clues. The sea holds me with that familiar sensation of being completely surrounded, cocooned. I slice smoothly through the water, my muscles remembering, despite my time out of training. I imagine surfacing to Mom's voice cheering me on; I couldn't see Mom in the crowd at swim meets, but I could always pick out her voice.

My heart thumps, and I feel dizzy at the memory. *Stop. Not now.*

I focus on the real sounds around me, on the science of it, on anything but Mom. Physics will tell you that sound travels farther in liquid, and it does—but our ears are made for air, and the sounds beneath the surface are muffled and unearthly. I blow out all my bubbles and tilt my head to suck in a really deep breath. Better.

Callum and I crisscross the entire lagoon, staring down from the surface and intermittently diving to scatter interweaving schools of metallic and technicolor fish. I'm petrified that at any moment the wrecked boat will loom out of the blue depths.

Deep Retreat. That was the name of Iona's boat. But it's impossible—the boat was too big to have entered the lagoon, and there's no sign of debris on the undulating seabed, only the occasional clump of seagrass or starfish.

When we reach the reef we swim alongside corals of all shapes and colors: round, purple and brain-like, huge feathery red ferns, knobbly yellow branches like witches' hands. The tropical fish that scatter before us are just as varied in color, shape, and size, and at any other time I'd be gawking in wonder, mesmerized. But all I'm interested in is finding my sister. Above the surface the tangled coral carcasses along the reef are bleached like bone and create an uneven barrier to the sea. Callum and I surface together at a break in the reef around four meters wide, forming a channel into the open ocean.

We bob in the current, and I suck in a deep breath, slip my goggles back on, and dive under. I hover by the gap where the sandy bottom gradually slopes away into the distance. The open-ocean side of the reef is lined with swaying fronds of brown seaweed, attached by large root systems to rocks at the base of the reef around six meters down. Callum swims closer to the seaweed grove, running his fingers through the ribbonlike fronds.

But my attention is out into the vast blue. He taps my shoulder and points at the seaweed, and I catch sight of a black tail disappearing.

We both surface.

"Did you see that? Reef shark," he says, eyes wide. "They aren't dangerous, but I think we should turn back."

I shake my head. I can't, not yet.

I dive again and kick down deeper, my ears popping as I scan the seabed. The sun is lower in the sky and stripes the top layers of water with shifting rays of gold and amber. Below that top layer is only blue; boundless, another world. No sign of the boat, so where is Poppy? How will I ever find her out there? I'm already desperate for breath, and I've only dived a couple of meters—

I freeze.

A shadow against the cobalt blue of the water ahead.

Star-shaped.

Person-shaped.

Poppy? Flooded with adrenaline, I swoop toward it. Bubbles blind me as I try to call out with my last huff of air.

The shadow sinks deeper. I stretch out, kicking hard. The figure spins and darts away into the far blue. My lungs are burning now, but I search frantically for another glimpse, then turn. I can't see the reef behind me. The bottom is many meters below, nothing but uniform blue ahead. I burst through the surface, gasping, as Callum slices through the water toward me.

"I thought . . . I thought I saw—"

I duck under and search again, then reality descends. It couldn't have been a person, not that deep, not swimming that fast. My panicking mind can't be trusted.

Callum's eyebrows knit together as he sculls backward toward the reef. "I don't think we should leave the lagoon just yet. Open-water predators can be big. Or there could be a rip current."

We swim back through the gap into the warmer lagoon waters, and I strike out for shore, scanning the seabed again, taking a long last look through the reef gap, willing Poppy to just *be there.*

We both wade out onto the beach and lean, hands on our thighs, as we get our breath back. Where to look for Poppy now? The rest of the island?

How is this happening? We should never have left London; less than a week ago we were at school.

Beti jogs down the beach to join us. Behind her in the trees a thin column of smoke rises.

"Did you see anything?" she says.

Callum shakes his head and chews on a thumbnail. Beti raises her chin. "I've got the fire started. We'll keep it burning so someone could spot the smoke."

The lagoon is where Beti surfaced from, so it seemed the obvious place to start looking, as I presumed Callum and I came from there too. But we can't presume anything. What if Poppy arrives in the lagoon—somehow—while I'm not there?

"We need emergency help," I say, trying to clear my mind, to think. I should be able to work out what to do; I'm good at problem solving. But panic has dulled my brain. I unzip the waist pack.

"Is there an emergency phone, signaling equipment?"

I already know the answer.

Callum shakes his head and starts along the beach, and Beti and I catch up.

"There are other islands. I saw them when we swam beyond the gap," he says.

It takes us a few minutes to reach the left end of the beach and climb a huge pile of boulders. There is no beach on the other side, just more rocks.

He's right. In the distance there's another island, hazy and indistinct.

"Maybe the others are on one of the other islands? This place is like an archi—What do you call it?" says Beti.

I stand on the highest rock and stare past the setting sun to the far side of the bay, where there is more haze, and a third island even farther away.

"An archipelago," I say.

"Yeah. Or one of those rings of islands," says Callum.

An atoll.

I chew my lip. So first we search this island, then we find a way to get to the other islands. My eyes scan over the water in the center of the atoll, but I can't allow myself to imagine what could be out there.

Beti, Callum, and I clamber down the rocks at the far side of the beach together.

"Wildhaven isn't a university study camp, is it?" I say.

Callum and Beti look at each other.

"We'll talk, but first we need to get a shelter set up before sunset," says Beti.

I follow them up the sand. My thigh muscles quiver from the swimming and climbing, and my head feels too heavy for my neck. Palm trees edge the beach and are widely spaced, creating a natural clearing for our camp. Beti now has an axe at her belt, and the fire she has built is large and surrounded by smooth rocks. Behind her is a pile of thick bamboo poles with pale, cut ends. She points to where she has marked a circle in the sand, and Callum starts to bang in one of the poles with a flat stone.

"Tell me what's going on . . . please? You can work at the same time, but you have to give me something."

She takes a deep breath and faces me.

"This isn't easy to explain. Iona met us all when she was treating our family members at refugee camps and hospitals in war zones. We are all orphans, or as good as. She offered us a test and found we had genetic markers for cancer. She was trialing a new therapy, and a complete way of life, outside society, at Wildhaven. She organized everything." As Beti talks, she sharpens the ends of the bamboo poles with a machete and hands them to Callum.

I blink at her. "How old are you both?"

"We are both fourteen."

Goose bumps rise on my arms. What was Iona *doing*?

"So what exactly is this therapy?" I say.

Beti shrugs. "It's an injection. You get a bit sick, as the therapy gets into your cells through a virus. We had two, one from Iona and then a booster from Dr. Jonathan. After that we were monitored by Iona. Dr. Jonathan used to test our blood, but even that's not needed anymore."

An injection. Like the injection she gave Poppy and me that seemed to cause the fever. Did we have this genetic marker? No one ever mentioned it to us before, but Mom died of cancer, and so did her mom. Anger builds in my chest, hot and tight.

"So this Dr. Jonathan might know where we are?" I say. Before the words have left my mouth, I doubt it. Poppy and I got a strong impression of what Iona thought of the doctor.

Callum bangs in another pole, and I see him catch his thumb and quickly straighten his face so Beti doesn't notice. "She said we would eventually have to relocate. Somewhere more remote. We weren't to discuss that with anyone, not even the doc."

Tears sting my eyes. I take a deep breath and wiggle my toes in the sand. The surface of the lagoon glistens, unbroken. *Where are you, Poppy?*

I watch as Beti directs Callum on where to place the rest of the poles and then holds them as he bangs them into the sand. They've already made a half circle. There are three palm trees that make up part of the walls, and I see how that will strengthen the hut. They know how to do this.

So my aunt took in the students at Wildhaven so she could test this experimental therapy on them.

"Were you allowed to leave the ecovillage? If you wanted to?"

"If people were coming and going then the camp would have soon been found, and we wouldn't have been able to stay there anymore," says Beti.

What was Iona thinking? She was a respected oncologist. What she was doing had to be illegal or it wouldn't have been so carefully hidden at Wildhaven. She must have gone to a lot of effort to get them all into the country.

"So Iona told you to lie to us about the natural lifestyles study?" I say.

Beti nods. "Just to hide the truth until you were ready. Sorry," she says.

I remember how no one really engaged us in conversation at Wildhaven, how they diverted our questions.

Callum clears his throat and rests the stone on top of the bamboo pole but doesn't meet my eyes. "Look, Aster, we were in bad situations when Iona found us. My dad and gran died in the same hospital months apart. Iona treated them. Then the house was sold to pay off some debts, and they wanted to put me in a children's home, so I lived on the streets for a bit. Iona heard, and she found me. Wildhaven was . . ."

"Our sanctuary," finishes Beti. "Iona found me in a refugee camp in France. I left Eritrea when I was ten. My mother was in the field hospital for months, I was alone, and I slept beneath her bed. No one cared what happened to me except Iona."

I am silent after that. They have no one, same as me and Poppy. No one is going to come looking for us. Any of us.

Callum smacks in another pole with a grunt. "The seaweed I was looking at near the reef is bullwhip kelp. We've learned how to prepare it to make fish traps and oyster cages. I am sure Iona planned for us to be here."

I remember the activities on the beach at Wildhaven.

"Look," says Beti, pointing inland, "there are breadfruit trees and a bamboo grove. Iona could have planted them."

I don't know whether this makes me feel better or worse, or whether I even believe them, because this sounds like wishful thinking to me. But it would be so, so good to believe they are right, that there is some sort of plan. Maybe Iona and Poppy are just on the next beach, with all of the others, together.

The low sun now stains the sand deep amber, dragging our shadows sideways, and the fire licks at the wood, kicking off heat. Beti and Callum start to bind the poles together with vines.

Frustration builds in me like a tight band around my ribs. We didn't sign up for this. Iona tricked us. Poppy and I aren't refugees or homeless—we have each other. We *had* each other. My fury flips, focusing inward. I should have trusted my instincts when Iona first said the house wasn't ready. I should have trusted Poppy when she said she wanted to leave. This is all my fault.

I can't just stand here. I turn away from Beti and Callum and stride through the trees and down onto the sand. I head to the other end of the beach—I guess it is the east end, opposite the setting sun—where we haven't explored yet. The boulders at the end look like a stack of stones inexpertly piled by a giant. It's a longer walk in this direction. I guess the entire bay is a couple of kilometers long. The sun is sinking fast, and I haven't searched hard enough. Before the end of the beach there's a stream, which flows out of the trees and down the sand, spreading into rivulets as it meets the sea. I taste it.

Fresh. At least that's something.

I finally reach the boulders and then scramble up a shallow cliff to stand on top and scan below. There's no beach on the other side, only more huge rocks all the way along the shoreline, rolling waves crashing into them at an angle. No one could have washed up here, surely—it doesn't bear thinking about. I turn back to the lagoon beach and spot Callum up by the trees, arms folded, watching me.

A breeze whips up as the red rind of sun drowns in the sea behind me. I jog back to the camp, and by the time I get there the moon is rising and nearly full, ribbons of pink scudding across it. More purplish clouds build along the horizon. It's all unbearably beautiful, and yet all I want is to be back in our tiny

London flat with Poppy. And Mom. My desperation winds tighter.

Callum and Beti have finished the round hut, a proper actual hut made out of bamboo. It is almost head-height, bound together with vines and roofed with palm leaves. Next to it is an open-sided palm-leaf canopy strung between the trees. Callum sits by the fire, prodding it with a stick, and Beti is cross-legged, hands moving quickly, weaving something.

"I found fresh water by the rocks," I say.

Callum punches the air, and Beti looks up and grins. I'm not interested in celebrating; all I want to do is carry on searching. I realize that both Callum and Beti are now wearing matching beige T-shirts and shorts and each has a machete strapped to their waist.

"Where did you get the clothes and equipment? Is there a flashlight?" I say. I unzip my waist pack and take out the items, laying them on the sand. A flint striker for lighting fires, a knife in a sheath, and three bundles of tightly rolled material that turn out to be a T-shirt, shorts, and a sort of sarong or sheet, all in the same sandy color.

"There's no flashlight," says Beti. She scans my face. "If you can find the right kind of stick, I can try to make you one with the fire."

She's kind, and my eyes prickle. I shake my head and pack the gear, along with the goggles around my neck, back into the equipment pouch. I keep the clothes out and strap the knife to my waist.

Beti hands me the life vest I was wearing when we arrived. The tubes still snake from the shoulders, ends dragging in the sand like dead tentacles.

"There's a pocket in the back; it holds a machete, a hatchet head, a hammock, and some other stuff," says Beti. "Enough to get us set up."

I stare at the black canvas-type fabric, finely woven with a slightly metallic sheen. Sewn into the back of the neck and the base of the back are vented black boxes. Next to the tubes there are holes, like empty sockets, where something has been plugged in.

This is all too much to take in.

I grind my teeth and rub my fingers across my forehead, feeling the grit of dried sea salt.

Callum looks up at me.

"We could all search the island, first thing tomorrow, together?" he says. I meet his brown eyes. He doesn't understand, neither of them do. I can't sit, I can't relax without Poppy.

"Aster. The life jackets seem to have motors inside them. Iona never mentioned anything like this, but I think it's what got us here safely. The others must have these same kits. They are safe too, just somewhere else. Another island, or another part of this one. Either way, Iona will find us."

I stare at Beti; her hands haven't stopped weaving grasses as she spoke. She seems to really believe this, but Callum bites his lip. Beti didn't see what she looked like when we pulled her out of the lagoon. Nothing about this is safe.

I turn away from them and stalk back to the beach, my eyes hot and gritty, my breath short. The moon is now obscured by clouds, and it is very dark. I sway in the breeze, surveying the inky lagoon, and press my knuckles to my teeth. Finally I sit until Callum and Beti's conversation behind me fades to murmurs. There's a shuffling sound at the fire, and then quiet.

An unnatural peace. The soft scrape of the sea against sand and the rustle of shifting palm fronds is a white noise, almost soothing. But like the gentle hissing of Mom's oxygen tank, it is a false comfort.

I don't know how much time passes before I'm aware of someone behind me. "Hey—here to relieve you. It's my watch."

Callum.

I shake my head. I can't. If I sleep it will be like giving up, like leaving Poppy out there, like accepting that no one else is coming.

Raindrops spatter us, then stop. Clouds scud across the full moon.

Callum offers a folded leaf to me, and at that moment the clouds pass and the bright moonlight highlights marks on his arm, puckered silvery circles on the inside of his elbow below his T-shirt sleeve. My eyes flick to his other elbow and see more of the same. Needle tracks?

He catches me looking, and I look away, feeling my brow furrow.

"You see why I didn't want to stay where I was. Gran and Dad's deaths—I never want to see anyone go through anything like that again." His voice is abrupt, gruff, and I get that.

"I'm sorry," I say. *I know.*

"Not your fault," he says, rubbing his thumb over the scars and then chewing the skin at the edge of his nail. "I know you think your aunt is mental, Aster. But I was one of the first at Wildhaven. She took me in; she got me clean. Then she made sure I won't go the same way as my family. Or the same way as other kids like me, with no one."

I don't say anything. I take the leaf from him, and there's food inside: pineapple, cooked bamboo shoots, and more coconut flesh. I eat it without tasting.

"Let me take my watch," he says, quietly. He chews on his thumb again, and although he's older than me, he doesn't seem it.

I swallow with difficulty. I know that without rest, anxiety will sweep me up and I'll be useless. The moon peers through the clouds and glitters on the lagoon, and its beauty mocks my despair.

"If you see anything at all—"

"I'll call out. Right away," Callum finishes.

I leave him wrapping the sheet of thin material around his shoulders as he settles in the dent I've left in the sand. I plod back to the hut. It is warm and gloomy inside, but I make out three pale hammocks attached to the trio of palm trees the hut was built around. They hang low to the ground, their cords crossing each other. One is occupied.

I unzip the gray suit and peel it down, and Beti tips from her hammock to help me yank it off my feet. I am blasted with a memory of Poppy. *We're on vacation, I smell sun lotion and fries, and Poppy's got gaps between her front teeth. She's lying on her back in hysterics as I haul a wet suit off her feet, dragging her along the sand . . .* The image makes me gasp, and my tears feel acidic, burning.

I leave the swimsuit on, and Beti hands me the soft T-shirt I took from the waist pack earlier. I draw a hitching breath and dry my face on the sheet she hands me. I'm hollowed out. I can't believe any of this is happening.

"Climb in," she murmurs, spreading out the fabric of a hammock.

I lie back, and the material folds over me as I rock. Beti climbs into her own hammock, and I maneuver awkwardly in the fabric to face the wall.

Where is Poppy now? I picture her in a hammock like I am, with Iona nearby, in control. I have to believe it.

I mouth the words: "Night, Popstar."

I imagine her voice: "Night, Astronomer." Then I press my face against the fabric and screw my eyes up tight.

I fantasize that this is all an elaborate trick or joke. Tomorrow the boat will pull up beyond the reef, and Poppy will be waving at me on deck, then shaking her head in horror at me because I'll be sobbing with relief.

My mind fights sleep but loses the battle. Between waking and sleeping, I speed back across the lagoon, through the gap in the reef, and into the blue beyond. Again I see that dark figure, that unmistakable star shape of a person twisting and kicking away. It's impossible, and yet I'm sure I saw it all the same.

9

The corridor of the hospice muffles my jogging footsteps with its carpeted floor, just as its lilac walls and watercolor prints are probably intended to muffle my grief and fear. The door of Mom's room is ajar, and I slide in, seeking out the heart monitor, which is drawing miniature moving mountain peaks. She's alive. The oxygen tank hisses, almost drowning out her crackly gasps, and a fine tube snakes over her shoulders from the toggle at her nostrils.

I tell my heart to slow down. Mom's propped up, mouth slightly open.

Her face has the sunken look I've grown used to, but the sculpted beauty of her features is still there, always, made more stark by her naked scalp. Her skin is pallid for her, an almost khaki brown against the white of the pillowcase. There is a shiny blotch on each sharp cheekbone. Are her breaths more shallow than usual? Is that even possible?

The message was to come straight to the hospice. Poppy is going for a sleepover tonight, so I don't need to worry about her.

"Hey—it's OK," says Suzie, Mom's usual nurse. "Sorry if I scared you. She has a temperature, and things looked a bit rocky earlier; her oxygen levels dropped. She's stabilized now and seems to be responding to antibiotics."

A fist clutches my heart. Another infection. The chemotherapy wasn't successful, and the lung cancer has now invaded Mom's whole body. There's not much else they can do.

Mom's eyes flicker. I move to her bedside and take her hand. That strong hand that used to nurse others, now almost skeletal, and so cold despite her fever. She grimaces, chest fluttering as she takes shallow sips of air. She's slowly drowning. It's agony for her to simply stay alive, let alone allow the morphine to wear off enough for her to interact with me. But she smiles, raises my hand to her lips, and kisses my knuckles. I lean over and give her a careful hug and a peck on the cheek. She still smells like my mom even through the illness and bleachy medical odor, and pain forms a tight ball at the base of my throat.

"All right, Mom?" I say, and the words feel dusty in my mouth.

But what am I supposed to say?

I know this is torture for her, and I hate that more than anything. But as always, I'm barely able to stop myself from sobbing and begging her not to leave us.

Mom nods at the writing pad on her bedside table, and I prop it up on the special sloped tray and put her pen in her hand. She lifts the pen, closes her eyes for a moment—gathering her strength—and scrawls:

Math test?

I had it this morning. I don't know how Mom always remembers. I roll my eyes because I know it comforts her if I act like I would at home.

"Seventy-six percent," I say.

Did u study?

I didn't, and I consider lying, but she'll know if I do. So I shrug. That's a good score, but not for me. I usually get top marks in math and science, and Mom's always fierce about Poppy and me not "wasting our talents."

She underlines the word "study" with a shaky line and points at me with the pen.

"Yes, Mom," I say. And I mean it. I can't disappoint her.

She's writing again.

Swim 7 p.m.

I almost laugh, then shake my head. Mom's insisted we keep going to school, carry on with our lives. But I can't compete in a meet, not tonight. It's a part of the championship I've been training for, but I couldn't care less now. She's far too ill for me to leave.

"No, Mom. I'm staying here. I'll read to you."

Mom frowns. Hand at her chest as if even feeling annoyance is too much for her disintegrating lungs. My own short breaths are heavy, noisy, a dreadful luxury. She points to her nose, her eyes full of concern, and I know what she means. I inhale through my nostrils, slowing my breathing, hating that Mom needs to worry about my anxiety when she is going through this.

She lifts the pen again and scribbles:

Bus. Go.

Her eyes grip me hard. She's still my mom, and the urge to do what she says is compelling, especially when it comes to swimming.

I hesitate. "I'll check with Suzie, OK?"

Mom gives the slightest nod.

Suzie says she is currently stable, but we know how things are.

I kiss Mom, and when I glance back, she's written more words and holds up the page, hand shaking with the effort. The letters are wobbly, but it is clear.

Reach. Kick. Breathe.

The words she used when she first taught me to swim, the words she called out from the side of the pool every time I raced. "It's all there is to it, girl. Reach your arms, kick your legs, and don't forget to—"

I wake, panting. I'm sweating, swaying, my body fighting the truth. Why can't I have a normal nightmare? Anything, no matter how scary, would be better than reliving the last time I saw Mom.

Blue light through cracks. Hammock. Hut. The island.

The hissing sound of Mom's oxygen tank still fills my head. I sit up and tip from the hammock. Poppy isn't here; I don't know where *here* is.

I force in deep breaths. Poppy is with Iona. She's safe, she has to be.

Beti and Callum snore softly in their hammocks. The sun isn't up yet, but I always wake early after years of swim training before school. I open the waist pack and strap the knife in its sheath to my belt, feeling sort of silly, as if I'm a character in a survival role-playing game. I pull the goggles over my head so they hang at my neck. The sandy floor of the hut is cold beneath my bare feet, and I shiver as the nightmare sweat cools on my skin.

My mind clings to the dream memory, Mom's rounded shaky handwriting forming her last words. The message that she'd slipped into a coma reached me at the pool less than two hours after I last saw her. I'd finished my races and was wrapped in a towel, surrounded by the rest of the squad, waiting for our times.

Reach. Kick. Breathe.

I hear her voice say it, and grief surges in my throat, behind my eyes. Mom never said, but I think she encouraged us to swim because her own mom died of lung cancer. She wanted our lungs as strong as they could be, and I happened to be good at it. She had mixed feelings about it, wanted me to do what I enjoyed but also see my friends and study hard. Could Mom somehow have known that we'd end up surrounded by the ocean? Could Iona have told her about Wildhaven?

I sneak out of the hut without waking the others and jog across the beach, quickly warming up. I climb the rocks at the east side of the beach, then decide to clamber along, try to reach the other side of the island. The sun is rising but not yet over the horizon, a bruise of blue light behind me. I move quickly, hopping from rock to rock with my bare feet. Finally I reach the end of the bay and am faced with a cliff. I clamber up and look out toward the ocean, noticing a dark blotch against the blue of the predawn sky. Another island, closer than the others we saw yesterday, which were hazy blurs in the distance. This one doesn't look like much more than a tangle of thick vegetation, and it wasn't visible from where we stood yesterday or from the sea at the lagoon gap. The water leading to it is paler turquoise; it almost looks like an underwater path, joining this island to the next bigger island with this outcrop between the two. I narrow my eyes, trying to judge the distance. I think I could swim to it. Maybe there'll be something else to see from there.

This place is tropical. Atolls are the remains of coral reefs after sunken volcanoes, but that doesn't give me much to go on as I think there are atolls in the Pacific, the Indian Ocean, and the Caribbean. The thought makes my heart plummet. Planes go down in the Pacific, and no one is ever found, even now, in modern times, with satellites and technology; it's that huge.

I climb back down and sit on the rocks, paddling my feet in the warm water. I shouldn't swim alone.

The sun rises, clearing the horizon much more quickly than it does at home, and as I'm bathed in golden light, my legs and arms buzz with the urge for activity. I should fetch the others, start searching the interior, but my brain is fogged up with my desperation to find Poppy. If we came out of the sea, I need to get back out there.

I'm still wearing the swimsuit I arrived in. I strip off the T-shirt and tuck it into a crevice in the rocks, take one last look at the small island from here, and make a ragged dive before I can change my mind.

At first I revel in the feel of the water. I follow the slight ridge, which is around four meters down. It's like a sandbar that joins our island to the smaller island, deeper water sloping off to either side. It seems safer in this shallower water where I can clearly see the bottom, and I try not to look off into the deeper blue on either side of it. Along the ridge there are thinly scattered rocks, coral carcasses, and a few patches of living coral, but nothing like a full reef. I swim past a field of spiky sea urchins to one side, waving their black spines like a gang of giant porcupines, then dive down to look closer at a clownfish colony darting in and out of a purple sea anemone, and almost gulp down water when a rock next to them moves. Color ripples across its surface, and when it unfurls a tentacle, I see it is a small octopus with a bulbous head around the size of a tennis ball. Swirls of red, white, and terra-cotta pulse over its skin. I've never seen anything look so much like an alien. It spreads all eight legs and creeps along the seafloor below me, then without warning forms an arrow shape and shoots off into the deeper blue nothingness.

I stop swimming for a moment to catch my breath. I've been so fascinated by the sea life that I didn't realize how far I've come. More importantly, how far there still is to go.

The small island is farther than it looks. I haven't done much open-water swimming, and although the sea is calm, the ripple of the waves means I'm using up my energy quicker than I would in the pool. My initial enthusiasm shrinks until I almost turn back at every stroke. This is reckless—my decision-making skills have been warped by my panicked state of mind—but I continue on, seeing nothing below me but the occasional school of fish.

The sun creeps higher in the sky. My muscles burn and anxiety rises, but it's now farther back than it is to the island I'm heading for. I could do with a rest before I turn back, and I really do want to get a look at the other island and beyond. The sun scorches the top of my head, and I dive under every few strokes to escape the heat. It's at least twice as far as I estimated. I must have swum around two kilometers.

At last I pull myself up on the thick roots that coat the rocks. The island seems to be nothing but a huge mass of mangrove trees perched on a pile of boulders. I make my way to a rock between the roots and sit and circle my shoulders, wincing at the ache and surveying my surroundings. A few young coconut palms rise from the center, but the dense canopies of mangrove surround them. I saw Callum drill into the dots on the top of a coconut with a blade, and I could give that a go; it would give me water and energy. The mangrove roots are everywhere, a gnarled overlapping lattice, some rearing up in front of me like giant claws. To reach the trees I need to either wind through the roots or climb over them, and that's going to use a lot of energy. But the thought of coconut makes my mouth water. I pause, tapping my fingers on my lips. I'm tempted to try to find some energy reserves and swim back right away. But I've made it this far; I should at least look around.

I scramble over the roots, and after a lot of effort I've made almost no progress and my bare feet are grazed raw by the rough bark. I might as well give up on finding a coconut. I stop to catch my breath, sweat staining the armpits of the now-dried swimsuit, salt drying crispy in my eyebrows. I lick my lips, parched. It's become too hot too quickly.

This could be the stupidest thing I've ever done. What if a

storm whips up? Or I twist my ankle? No one will ever know what happened to me, and I'll die here. I look behind me. I can't even explore the rest of this island because it's only going to make me even more dehydrated.

I climb into a large gap between the boulders and sit for a moment, my back against a rock, partly shaded by a mesh of tree roots above me. Something in the corner of the hollow catches my eye.

A shape I recognize. Pale, misshapen. A hand.

My heart leaps into my throat. I gasp and press my back against the rock, heart racing, even as I see it isn't a hand but the remains of a glove.

I hold my chest, slowing my breathing, my eyes fixed on the glove. I crawl over to it and pull it out from where it's pinched between two rocks encrusted with mussels. It rips a little on the sharp shells but comes free. I hold it up to the sunlight. It is definitely a glove but missing the whole palm and two of the fingers, the rest barely more than a rag. It's rotted and mildewed, green and slimy in parts, but a couple of patches are gray, which might have been its original color. It's made from a thin, stretchy material like our suits, and I hold it against my swimsuit. It's a much lighter gray.

It's only an old glove, lost at sea, nothing to do with us. I slip it under my waist belt as I have nowhere else to put it. I try to shrug the feeling off, but I keep imagining it *was* a hand, something awful to do with Poppy. No. I won't start jumping at shadows and freaking out. I can't.

Need to get out of here, now.

I scramble from the hollow too quickly with an inexplicable feeling something is following me. I stumble and take a giant step to regain my balance but miss the next rock and go down hard on my knees.

When I haul myself up, a jolt of hot pain forces me to cry out. A sharp ridge on the rock is smudged with my blood. I shudder and stand, wincing, looking down at my knee.

Oh God.

The cut is about the length of my thumb. I bend my knee a little to get a better look and start back as the wound opens, revealing the white of the deeper layers of my flesh within, like an open mouth drooling blood. This is bad, so bad. A determined trickle of red already tracks down my shin. I look around me for something to bind it with, but there's nothing. I'm such an idiot.

I'm not at the same place I climbed out of the water; here it is all tree roots. Toppling from root to root, I leave a trail of oily blood smudges on the bark. The roots bounce and sway over the water, and at last I get to a place where I can dive in. I haul air right to the bottom of my lungs and crouch. A dark drop of my blood hits the water and curls into brown tendrils against the blue.

I breathe in through my nose, out through my mouth. *Three in, six out.* As soon as I get my breath back, I'll swim. I'm spooked, that's all. It was just a glove, too old to be anything to do with us.

Don't think about it anymore.

Reach. Kick. Breathe.

I blank her voice out, look down at the wound again, and reason that I'm not badly hurt—the cut only gives off a dull throb. Counting my breaths for a few more rounds helps me feel calmer. I straighten and circle my arms; my muscles aren't as tired as I thought. Our island is now surrounded by a sea haze and looks alarmingly far away.

Well, not for long. I squat, preparing to dive, toes dipping into the water.

I blink in disbelief.

A triangular fin gleams blackly as it cuts a steady line through the water toward me.

I scramble back up the branches, gasping. Below me, the blood from my cut has billowed into a murky cloud. The fin whips back and forth, churning eddies and whorls topped with pink foam.

Shark.

10

Rays of light slice through the vertical blinds and highlight the dust motes Sam has been watching while he waits for Granda to wake up. The hospital room is stale and stuffy, but the window's jammed shut—he's tried it twice. He checks his watch and sighs. He doesn't like to wake him, but visiting hours will be over soon, and they are pretty strict even though this is a private room. The heart monitor shows a steady beat, and the oxygen mask is wrapped around the tank, unused. Good signs that

Granda is fighting off the infection. He looks a lot better than when Sam saw him last, less sunken.

A knock at the door, and a man enters without waiting for an answer. He's wearing an open-collared blue shirt and a stethoscope around his neck.

"I'm sorry," he says, "I'll come back."

He turns as if to leave, but Sam stands, the hospital chair making a squeaking sound against the linoleum.

"No worries. I'm his grandson. You can carry on with me here, Granda won't mind," he says.

"It's quite all right, take your time," says the doctor. He has a slight accent, clipped and correct, and is Sam's dad's age with dark hair flanked by wings of silver at the temples. But it's his eyes that catch Sam's attention. Pale green-blue. He flashes Sam a smile as he leaves, and instantly Sam is taken back to the fire site in the bush. The same guy—

A rattling cough. Sam turns back to the bed to find Granda awake and trying to shuffle himself into a sitting position.

"What are you doing, boy?" he says. "Bad enough one of us has to be here."

Sam supports Granda's back and adjusts the pillow.

"Good to see you too, Granda." He smiles. "Feeling any better?"

"Still sick, but the nurses are happy with me."

"That's really good, Granda." He hesitates, then points at the door. "That doctor—?"

"Oh, him?" says Granda, and closes his eyes for a moment. "I don't suppose it matters anymore."

He clears his throat, and his eyes are bright as they meet Sam's.

"He ran the treatment trial I was on—Marisogen—but it was never licensed. He . . . visits when I'm in hospital, asks some questions, gives me a once-over."

"Is there a chance you could go back on the trial, then?" says Sam. Hope rises in his chest, sickly sweet.

Granda shakes his head.

"I wish I could. Marisogen was the only treatment that actually worked, and it didn't even have side effects. Just an injection every two weeks."

"What's this doctor's name?"

"Nygard." Granda breaks off into a coughing fit and points to the oxygen. Sam fixes the mask on his face and turns the valve, and Granda rolls his eyes as his breathing eases. Sam remembers how his granda recovered so well on this Marisogen when he was staying with Mom. Since then, the cancer has been held in check by chemotherapy, but his lungs are damaged, and he's always catching infections. This last one was particularly bad.

The nurse arrives, and Sam is kindly reminded of visiting

hours. Sam squeezes Granda's hand and says goodbye, lingering at the door until Granda bats him away.

As he unlocks his bike, Sam recalls the fire site in the bush. Could this Dr. Nygard really be the same guy? He scans the parking lot and wonders whether he should go back in, try to find him. But what would he say? As he rides home, memories flood in.

The girls from the plane. Poppy and Aster.

Sam pedals faster. He wants to find out more about this doctor.

Back at home he calls out a greeting to his parents in the living room and heads straight to his room. He's experiencing that same odd, unbalanced feeling—the dull pounding in his temples and clenching of his stomach—that he often has after visiting Granda. But this time it's more than that. Why wasn't Marisogen licensed if it worked so well?

Sam wonders if he should tell his parents. Mom never liked how secretive that trial was. But what if this doctor is planning a new trial or something and telling his mom stops it going ahead? He can't get his head around this. In the end, he calls the hospital, and they confirm Dr. Nygard isn't part of the oncology team treating Granda but is a consultant in genetic disorders who runs a clinic a couple of times a month at the hospital. Sam asks to speak to Granda, but he's asleep.

The girl's cell phone. How could he have forgotten? The

police had sent the girl's phone back to him. That's what they did with unclaimed lost property.

Sam opens the wardrobe in his bedroom. He shifts aside two pairs of old sneakers. Underneath is a shoebox with *Random Stuff* scrawled across the lid in marker. Inside, underneath gig tickets, receipts, and a broken watch, is a brown envelope. Sam draws a deep breath and tips the phone and a ball of tissue out onto his hand.

The phone charges fine, but Sam still can't find a way to hack into it, same as when he first found it. It feels heavy in his hand. He checks again, but every website still states that the email address is required. Finally he gives up trawling online phone forums and spins around on his desk chair with a dramatic groan. He taps the phone screen, and a background of turquoise water appears with the security dot grid on top. Water. He remembers that when Poppy had said her older sister was a champion swimmer, Aster had smiled for the first time, embarrassed. Sam keeps looking at the screen as if it is going to tell him something.

The back is encased in a rubber skin with a faded rainbow pattern. Sam flips it over and peels off the rubber case. Nothing on the smooth metallic back. He slots his thumbnail under the casing and opens it to reveal the battery. Sam blows out a breath. This is so pointless. It's late. He's working tomorrow—

His heart skips a beat. Yes! The phone has an SD card tucked above the battery. His first ever phone had one of these little storage cards to back up photos before everyone used the cloud. He slides out the card with the edge of his stubby thumbnail. His laptop is a few years old and has a selection of slots on the side.

The SD card fits in one of the slots. Sweet. Sam opens the folder, and sure enough there are two folders, one labeled Photos, one Camera Uploads. He hovers the cursor over a yellow folder icon, and his stomach churns. This is the girl's private stuff, but surely she won't mind if it helps him get her phone back to her? There could be photos on here that aren't backed up. He clicks the photos folder open and starts scrolling through the photo roll. It's a shock to see the older girl again. Aster, with the deep-bronze skin and curls the same color. She looks even sadder than he remembers.

Sam skips through the shots. Some selfies. Aster with two other girls outside a movie theater—her smile is closed-lipped, and they are laughing, hugging her. He wonders if that was when her mom was still alive. Further back there are more, definitely of her mom; some are in the hospital, and the woman wears a headscarf and has an oxygen tube beneath her nose. She looks too young to be so ill. Sam can't imagine how grim it would be to see his own mom like that. Granda is bad enough. He doesn't search any further back, closes the folder. He clicks open the camera uploads.

Sam is startled by his own face. In the selfie he is above the girls, leaning over their headrests and tucking his tangled blond hair behind his ear. Poppy is pouting as she drags Aster into the shot.

The next photo is of the sign for Tokomaru Bay that Poppy sent him.

The following shot causes Sam to reel back from the screen. It's slightly out of focus.

The ecovillage *did* exist.

Groups of young people sitting cross-legged on mats. They seem to be crafting things, woodworking and weaving. The back of a girl's head blocks half the screen; there are flowers in her hair. Behind her is a large shelter of some kind with wooden joists holding it up. In the far background, there's the edge of what looks like a wooden cabin and trees.

The next photo is blurry again, and he guesses it was snapped very quickly. A girl and a boy holding a one-handed plank pose. Another photo seems to be of the interior of a hut, but all he can see is the window—everything else is too dark. The last shot is of a man talking to a woman who has her back to the camera, which is focused on the man's face. Sam stares.

It's him.

Dr. Nygard *was* the man at the fire site, and he'd been *at* the ecovillage. So why had he acted like he didn't know it existed, scraping around in those ashes?

Sam swings back around on his desk chair, scrubs his fingertips into his hair and flattens it again.

He clicks open his email and copies in the email address of the hospital where Granda is staying and writes a header: "Attn Dr. Nygard, Genetics Clinic." What should he say?

Dear Dr. Nygard,

I saw you at the hospital today and would appreciate your help. Fraser Banks is my grandfather and

Sam pauses, unsure how to continue. Keep it brief.

he speaks highly of you. I wonder if we could talk?

Thanks so much for your time,

Sam Banks

Sam reads the message back, hovering his cursor over the send button. He remembers the way the older girl's eyes had met his as he waved goodbye at the airport. When he'd looked up their names, he found out an aster was a purple daisy. Named for a flower like her sister.

Aster said their mom died of lung cancer. Granda's cough fills his head.

Why was a doctor of genetics at a fire site near the place where Poppy had left her phone?

Sam shakes his head because it is all so . . . strange. He could be making connections where there are only coincidences. He unwraps the piece of glass from the tissue. He didn't know what it was the last time he'd looked at it, but now he recognizes it from chemistry class. It is the broken base end of a test tube. The outside is blackened by the fire, but inside there is a dark brown residue. It flakes off on the tip of his finger.

Could it be blood?

He quickly brushes off his finger in disgust and drops the glass fragment back on the tissue. He stares at it, then back at the email, and clicks send.

11

I scramble back across the roots and find a shady spot beneath them to perch, watching the shark fin trace lazy lines back and forth across the surface of the water. It's already after midday. I'm really thirsty now and sweating, even in the shade. I don't dare think about how bad my situation really is. I can't panic, not now.

The dark triangle dips and disappears, and I hold my breath, praying for it to be gone. But it surfaces again a few seconds later, orbiting more slowly, as if it knows it is only a matter of time before I'm forced into the water.

I'm not going to waste my energy yelling for help—the island's way too far away—but I scan the horizon anyway, and my eyes catch on something tiny, dark, moving. When I blink there is nothing there but more sea. No one is coming, no one knows where I am. The sun is bright, and my eyes water, blurred. I must have imagined I saw something.

I've no idea what I'm going to do. I can't swim leaking blood, because the shark—or another one like it—will soon be back.

Think. Problem solve. My blood brought it here.

I need to block the scent of my blood. Cover the wound. I gather some fallen palm fronds draped over the mangrove roots, trying to pick ones that aren't seriously rotten. I could pack the wound with these, then wrap it? I shudder at the idea but can't come up with anything better.

I'll have to make do with what I've got to bind it up. I look at the moldering glove tucked into my belt and grimace. My knife. The only other thing I have is my swimsuit; I'll have to make it work. I stand out of view of the beach, behind a tree, and check that I'm alone—stupidly, as I've never felt more alone in my life—then pull down the high-necked swimsuit and hack strips from the back. The bottom half of the swimsuit is designed like cycling shorts, and I saw the legs off all the way around so

I have two stretchy loops. I pull it back up. It now gapes at the back but just about covers me.

The blood is already congealing in the cut. I wad one of the softer leaves into a kind of pad and take a deep breath. *Here goes.* I mash it right into the cut, gritting my teeth with a moan. I wrap the fabric strips around to hold it in place, and after a few tries my knee is firmly bandaged in gray swimsuit material. I feel a rush of hope. It throbs, but the swimsuit material is stretchy and thick. This could work.

I follow my dried blood smears down to the place I last saw the shark and peer down into the water. No sign of the shark. But how will I know if it has really gone? I wait in the glaring sun, wiping the sweat from my hairline, feeling more trickle down my spine. If only I knew more about sharks, like how persistent they are.

I could tread water here and wait to see if it reappears. I'll stick close to the branches so I can haul myself out really quickly if it comes. If it is still around, I'll have to wait until tomorrow morning.

Staying the night on the mangrove island feels like a terrible plan.

I need to try this.

I edge out onto a sturdy root that leads right into the water, snap on my goggles, and dip in my toes. Nothing comes. I sit on the root and sway my legs in the water, easing lower until the water covers the wound, my heart racing in my throat. I cling to the root until the water is up to my armpits. I'm panting and start to count my breaths.

One, two, three in . . .

I don't know how big that thing is, or how fast.

One, two, three, four, five, six out . . .

It could bite me in half before I even see it.

Come on. Breathe.

Reach. Kick. Breathe.

I draw a deep breath and duck under.

A dark shape speeds toward me from the blue.

I haul myself up, the root bouncing. My arms strain as I swing myself up and over, folding my body over the root. I scramble one leg up, then the other—I'm out. I lie on my belly along the root, panting, dripping, coughing and gasping. Out. Alive. Not trusting myself to move, I press my cheek to the bark and wait for my heart to slow. The shark can't get me here. I'm safe. I'm safe. That was not a good plan. Far too close.

Raising my head, I scan the water, frowning. No fin.

I look directly down and glimpse something moving in the blue below, but I can't make it out. I peer closer.

It's gone. But it looked like a . . . face. Can't be. Must have been a fish or something.

I squeeze my eyes shut tight and then open them and scan the water again. This time I am unable to tear my eyes away.

A boy's face, underwater. Wide eyes stare up at me. Dark hair sways. A purple mark passes through his eyebrow and down his cheek.

Not a fish.

I cling to the root, blinking. His face hovers a few centimeters below the surface. He is really there, but where did he come from? Is he from the camp too?

He's so still, and his eyes look strange, pale. A horrible thought hits me. Is he . . . *dead*?

Lifting onto my hands and knees, my whole body trembles.

His hand bursts from the water. I almost tip sideways from the root. His fingers make a shooing gesture, and I twist into a crouch and scuttle back.

The boy's hand sinks back below.

I stare at the water where he was. Silence aside from my ragged breaths. The ripples dissipate.

Where is he now? I scan the water all around. He didn't have scuba gear or a snorkel. The sea is flat. My heart thumps so wildly I'm sure I have no sense of time, but he has definitely been down there longer than a breath.

I can't make sense of it. I scratch around for a reasonable explanation.

The shark. The shark must have . . . oh God. I should have warned him about the shark.

I lean forward again, peering down, terrified of what I might see, and then stumble back as the boy's head and shoulders break the surface. He shakes his head like a dog with water in its ears, a deep vertical crease between his brows. He blinks repeatedly and seems to have trouble focusing on me.

"You need to get out of the water, there's a sh-shark," I say.

The root I'm balancing on sways. The boy studies me, head to one side, eyes raking over my face and body, as I gaze at him, openmouthed. His skin is darker brown than mine with a cool, sallow tone.

When I meet his gray eyes, he dips his chin. His brows are as thick and black as his hair, and they arch expectantly, but his mouth is closed, silent.

I edge forward. He shakes his head.

He ducks and disappears.

I wait. He's gone again.

Only one explanation. This boy is a hallucination.

I've been gassed in a boat, marooned on an island, swum far too far, and been hunted by a shark. I've probably got sunstroke, I'm definitely dehydrated, and I might have lost a lot of blood. Oh—and I'm grieving my mom, have an anxiety disorder, and have just recovered from a fever. It would be weirder if I *weren't* hallucinating.

But I wait. The sun has now passed over the island, so I'm in shade. There's barely any afternoon left. I watch the water.

No shark. No boy.

Stupid mind. It's been a long time since I saw the shark now, and the sun set quickly last night—I don't have time for imaginary sea boys. Checking my knee, I find no sign of blood and tell myself to forget the waking daydreams and get back to the plan. I ping my goggles back into place and lower myself into the water more quickly this time. I scan below.

The boy speeds up to me from the deep and hangs motionless around two meters below me.

I fight the urge to whip out my knife as I float on the surface staring down at him.

He seemed boyish when I could see only his head above the water, but now it's clear he's powerfully built, and his expression isn't exactly friendly. There's something familiar about him, the way he tilts his head and holds my gaze, but I can't have seen him before—he's impossible.

He's not wearing goggles.

And he's a lot better armed than I am.

The boy grips a jagged dark blade in one hand, there's a longer blade strapped to his thigh, and a spear juts over his shoulder. Plaited straps cross his chest, and tied at each shoulder is a translucent globe around the size of a tennis ball that flickers faintly violet against the darker water below.

His chest is bare. And the top half is slashed with fine lines. I frown, confused. Three lines on each side, sloping up diagonally from the center between well-defined pecs. Are they tattoos? As I stare, they gently shift open a fraction, then close. In a rhythm.

I can't look away.

That rhythm, that ripple of movement in his chest, is the boy breathing.

Breathing . . . water.

Gills. The word springs to mind. He is breathing water. Through *gills.*

The boy tilts his head and drifts up toward me, and I know I'm right even though this is so very very wrong. There's no other way he could be underwater for so long.

I thrust my knife out in front of me, aware that I have no real idea what to do with it. My metal blade glitters as I bob in the surface swell, bubbles slipping from the corner of my mouth. The edge is sharp, but the weapon stupidly small, only the length of my palm. His gaze traces a triangle between my knife, my eyes, and my neck and chest. The boy's gray eyes are lighter beneath the water, but the pupils are tiny and jet-black. My goggles are fogging. I want to climb out but don't want to turn my back on him.

I tilt my head and gulp the air, keeping the knife out in front of me. When I turn back, the boy is still there in the same position a meter or so below me. His eyes rest on my blade, then track back to my face, and he raises his eyebrows.

He drifts up, toward me, hands raised as if approaching an

injured animal likely to bite. Pointing at my injured knee, he bares his teeth, widens his eyes, and makes a fist, which he thrusts toward the open sea. Then he indicates my leg again, shakes his head, and points up at the surface.

Strangely, I totally get what he is saying. Danger, my wound, he wants me to surface. And then what?

I look down at my leg and shake my head. I tap my chest and point in the direction of the island we arrived on.

He bares his teeth again. I scull back. He could be indicating I'm in his territory or something and he wants me out. Maybe this boy *is* the danger. He can't be anything to do with the camp. He's—I don't know *what* he is.

When he darts away, I am buffeted in his wake, and I watch his underwater stroke in amazement. Hands palm-up at the base of his back, he holds his legs tightly together and pumps them up and down in a double kick, his body undulating, streamlined through the water. I've never seen a human swim underwater as fast or as fluently. Even my swim coach would be impressed. He disappears into the turquoise blue ahead of me, gone.

I'm questioning what to do next when the boy streams back like an arrow, right up to me. He holds out a swath of green seaweed, translucent as tissue paper, swaying in the current, and swims so close that I kick away from him. He jabs a pointing finger at my knee, then at the seaweed, then back to the surface.

Shakily, I ease the knife back into the sheath strapped at my waist, my eyes never leaving his. I start to point to the island again, but he falls still, his head flicks, and then he darts toward me, grasps my upper arms, and propels me upward. I shoot through the surface, outraged by the sudden contact and shocked by his strength.

I drag myself back onto the branches again, then scoot back, and the boy reaches up with powerful arms to grasp the root above him. I see his chest gills fully displayed as dark slashes across his pecs, streaming water for a few seconds before closing flat. Then he heaves up his muscular body and clings to the branch with his legs, hanging upside down. The root bends beneath his weight and rocks wildly. It could be funny—in completely different circumstances.

I scan the water. I don't see a fin, but that doesn't mean there isn't a shark down there.

The boy hauls himself up with some difficulty and wobbles, legs bent and bowed, head tucked low into his shoulders. He's as ungainly here as he was graceful in the water. For a few moments he stays hunched over, eyes screwed tight, both hands covering the slits across his chest.

Uncurling a little, he rises into a crouch and removes one hand from his chest to balance on the mangrove root. He peers down at his chest—his . . . gills—with his jaw clenched and twitching. The slits are now closed and much less noticeable, narrow dents in his skin. He runs his fingers across them, fear etched on his face.

I clear my throat.

"Are you—OK?" I say.

The boy untucks his chin from his chest and blinks rapidly.

He glances toward the sun, loses his balance, and pitches backward. Without thinking, I reach out and grab his hand. He grips tight, his skin surprisingly warm. He waves at the sky and shields his eyes. He's dazzled by the sun. How long has he been underwater?

His large hand still encloses mine, as if I'm anchoring him in a gale-force storm.

This is so surreal. Beyond surreal.

My eyes flick to his hands and feet. No webbing. His body is normal.

Apart from his *gills*.

A drip escapes from the corner of one of the dents on his chest and tracks down his tight stomach, and I realize that just like I held air in my lungs underwater, he seems to be holding water in his lungs. If he even *has* lungs.

A human. Who can't breathe on land. Maybe he's never been above the surface.

His grip on my hand remains tight as he stares about him, then checks his chest again.

His outfit doesn't help me get a fix on where he came from.

He's wearing sort of cutoff cargo trousers in faded blue, and one leg ends mid-thigh and has been repaired with thick, dark twine. A red-handled hunting knife is strapped above his knee with the same twine. The other trouser leg finishes at the knee and still has two thigh pockets that bulge. The buttons have been replaced with shells with holes through the middle. The band he's using as a belt seems to be a purple luggage strap with pale letters running around it, tied in a knot at his waist. A few black pouches hang from the plaited leathery straps that cross his chest. The glowing globes that floated at his shoulders underwater now flop forward like deflated balloons, and I can see where they are tied on. They must be filled with bioluminescent algae or plankton or something. I remember Iona's ruse to get us on board her gassing boat and shake my head, wanting to dislodge the memory.

Finally he looks back at me. He reaches out and, although I flinch, touches the material of my swimsuit at the shoulder. He points to me, to himself, and then to the island, and narrows his eyes as if calculating.

I don't have a clue what he means, so I shrug.

Still cringing as though the light is painful, he holds up the seaweed and indicates my wound again. I think he wants to help me, and I don't know what else to do. When I edge back along the branch to the rocks, he follows, head to one side, unfolding from his crouch enough to stagger.

My heart pounds. I should talk to him instead of gawping like an idiot.

"My name's Aster."

His mouth is a tight line, but his head juts forward. He tilts his chin back to survey me.

"Can you hear me? Do you speak English?"

He nods, once for each question.

I blink. "Can you talk?"

A nod for yes, a shake for no. He points to me, then back to himself, pressing his lips together so tightly they are colorless. Raising his eyebrows, he shakes his head as though weary, then scrambles back across the roots and dives into the sea.

12

While the boy is back underwater, presumably breathing, I crouch for a few moments, trying to process what I've seen. He understands me but doesn't speak. His lungs are full of water, and air needs to pass through your vocal cords to make a sound, so he *can't* speak. The shadowy figure I saw yesterday—underwater, beyond the reef—could have been this boy.

A cold feeling creeps across my skin again. What if he is the reason the other students aren't on the island?

I shouldn't let myself believe he wants to help me. Just because he hasn't hurt me doesn't mean he won't, so I draw my knife again and watch my knuckles whiten around the hilt. When I hear him splash back out of the water, my heart thumps. He stumbles along the roots toward me like a drunk person, and I scoot backward a little when he collapses into a crouch next to me, dripping. He shifts his feet around until he is able to keep his balance. His frown casts his eyes in shade, and his lips press tightly together.

I speak slowly, clearly. "Have you seen others like me? Without . . . your . . ." I indicate his gills and then my chest. A rushing sound fills my ears as I brace myself for him to communicate something devastating about Poppy.

His eyes widen and his nostrils flare as his neck thrusts forward. I raise my hands, palms up. Clearly I said something wrong. He shakes his head, then holds up two fingers and points to our island, then adds another finger and jabs it at me.

"Only the two on the island and me? Are you sure? I'm looking for my sister."

He shakes his head, frowning, then makes a cutting movement with his hand, and I get the strong impression he doesn't want to answer any more questions. At least, I hope that's what he's trying to say. I frown back at him and square my shoulders.

"My sister is only eleven. I need to find her."

The boy looks away and gives another smaller shake of his

head, then he gestures abruptly for me to sit. He points at my knee, his jaw clenching.

He can't do a worse job of it. The wound hasn't stopped throbbing. He lifts the seaweed from where it is clumped on the rocks and raises his eyebrows.

"Is that going to help my wound? Will it stop the shark scenting me?" I say.

A nod.

I can't get back to the island chased by sharks. I also can't see how that piece of seaweed is going to make any difference, but he seems at home in the water and hasn't been eaten by sharks himself, so he's probably my best shot. I sit, and under the boy's direction, unwind the strips of swimsuit fabric, wincing as I peel the wadded material from the cut and it wells with fresh blood. He folds himself almost in half to scrutinize the cut up close, then shakes his head as if he doesn't approve.

I want to tell him it wasn't exactly deliberate but keep quiet.

He strides back across to the sea and fills a black pouch with water, then pours it over the wound, cleaning it. It smarts, and I take a sharp intake of breath. He reaches into another pouch tied to a strap across his chest and brings out fingers coated in transparent greenish gel.

The boy pauses as if sizing me up. His face twists into a grimace: eyebrows arched upward, a flash of teeth. I don't know what he means.

He grips my leg firmly below the knee, and I gasp at the sudden skin contact but am immediately distracted because when he slathers the cold gel into the wound it's as if thousands of wasps are stinging me in unison. The wave of pain shoots up my leg; I screech, and when I kick out at him, he restrains my ankle with his other hand. My back arches, and sweat prickles my scalp. I lunge forward and grip his forearm with both my hands, squeezing tight and grinding my teeth. As suddenly as it began, the torment is replaced by a cool tingling, and the squawk in the back of my throat strangles off. I wipe tears from the corners of my eyes with a trembling hand and look down.

The boy's fingers pinch the wound closed.

He holds my gaze as my breath slows, and when a smile curls the edge of his closed lips, I glare at him.

"That really *really* hurt!"

He tentatively moves his fingers aside, and I lean forward, amazed. The wound holds, all that is left is a slim dark line. As the boy turns back to the sea, I stare at my leg, then at his back in amazement. He dives.

When the boy returns, he crouches by my side again and slicks the translucent seaweed he first offered me over the wound. Immediately it tightens, like one of those peel-off face masks, as it dries to my skin. With the side of his thumb, he smooths the surface of the weed, easing out any air bubbles from underneath. Now that he isn't causing me intense agony,

I notice that his movements are gentle, his fingers long. He's very close, the top of his head below my chin. From this angle, he's just a boy. His hair stands up in glossy black tufts, shorter at the front and sides but thick and long at the back, wet clumps clinging to his shoulders. Not a style many boys could get away with since the 1970s, but he pulls it off and I guess it keeps the hair out of his eyes when swimming. There are three more furrows in the skin on his neck, curving behind his ear. Gills.

He smells salty and boyish but not unpleasant: wet skin drying in the breeze. Normal.

So *not* normal. A boy who breathes underwater. Sea Boy.

"I guess I should thank you," I say, "despite the agony."

He raises his eyebrows and shrugs as if to say, "That would be nice," and I find myself smiling.

"Can I—safely swim back now?"

He leans back and screws up his nose, as if dubious that I can do it.

I don't appreciate the look.

"I swam here fine, and I need to swim back," I say.

I stand. He reaches out toward my neck, tipping his head to one side, and I duck back. He taps behind his ear, and I get it. My hair is still in the high, messy bun I knotted before I swam, but a lot of strands have come free, and I move them aside to show him my neck.

"I don't have . . . them," I say. "Are they . . . gills?"

He meets my gaze. The storm-cloud gray of his eyes is striking against his skin color, but they don't look so strange now, above the surface.

His expression is guarded, thoughtful, and I feel like he's torn about something. The light beyond the island's shadow is a rich late-afternoon orange. I do not want to swim back in the dark. He taps his chest, points at me, then indicates the island in the distance. He dives. I don't have a lot of choice but to follow this Sea Boy. After one last glance down at my knee, I shake my head and plunge into the ripples he has left.

13

I surface to snap my goggles into place. Sea Boy drifts below me. He makes a clicking sound, and by the way his jaw moves, I guess it comes from his back teeth.

A massive fish sweeps in front of us, triangular wings blasting me with turbulence. I blow out all my bubbles at once and dart behind Sea Boy, my mind screaming *shark* even as I realize he isn't fazed at all. I steady myself with a hand on his shoulder and peer around him. A manta ray. I recognize it from nature documentaries. The fish is three times my size with a huge toothless cavern of a mouth probably capable of swallowing me whole. Strange prominences curve out below its wide-spaced eyes; it is black with white patches on top and fully white underneath and has a tapered, black tail. It nudges the boy's stomach with its flat head, and he strokes its gills, chattering his back teeth together.

Brown seaweed threads around the fish's head and the back of its wings, like a harness.

Oh no.

Sea Boy grips the rein above the manta ray's head and slips his feet beneath a strap under its long, spiked tail.

He intends us to *ride* it?

I give him a wide-eyed look. Seriously?

Sea Boy clicks his teeth again, and the manta ray speeds off with him pressed tight against its back, weaving from side to side then shooting into the distant blue before banking sideways and streaming back toward me. I choke as it carves right by me, spinning me in its wake, and I surface, spluttering. The sun is sinking, the sea glitters amber, and I know the island is too far to reach alone before dark. Above water I'm in deep trouble. Below, a boy is breathing seawater and riding a giant manta ray. I inhale deeply, then dive again.

Sea Boy guides the giant fish lazily back and forth. He gestures for me to come closer.

I swim over, and he drifts so I am floating above him. What am I doing? He adjusts the spear at his back so it rests to the side, and when he indicates for me to hold on to him, I wonder if I catch a glimpse of shyness in his expression. I shake my head in disbelief at what I am doing, then scull down, breathing out some bubbles to decrease my buoyancy. I rest against the boy, my stomach to his spine, and before I can register the closeness as awkward, the manta ray flaps its wings and I am forced to hug Sea Boy's waist tight or be left behind. Hooking my legs around his, I glue my cheek between his shoulder blades as the huge fish accelerates through the water. It is exhilarating and terrifying.

When my lungs beg for air I raise my face, tap Sea Boy's stomach with my fingers, and he directs the manta ray to skim along the surface just long enough for me to splutter a breath before swooping back below. We continue like this, and he soon anticipates the length of time between breaths before I have to tell him. Finally we slow down and I unlock my muscles, relieved. At the speed we've been traveling, we must already be at the island. But when I raise my head, I'm faced with a cloud of pale balloons and spiraling tentacles. I snort out a few bubbles in dismay.

Jellyfish.

The swarm stretches in both directions as far as I can see, blocking our way. Only the two meters directly above the seafloor is clear of them.

Sea Boy gestures with an open palm for me to wait. *Well, obviously.* I shoot to the surface for a breath and scan around. The island is now so near I can see individual rocks. I spin in the water, and my gaze catches on a dark blotch behind me, in the direction we just came from. Up on the surface the waves are choppy. I remember I also saw something when I was at the mangrove island. A boat? A swimmer?

I tread water more rapidly, trying to raise myself higher out of the water to get a better look, but there's nothing to see. I imagined it, or it was a piece of driftwood. I duck under and stare in that direction, but the visibility is worse below and there is nothing but that dizzying blue. Sea Boy sweeps out from underneath the jellyfish and toward me, indicating a short distance between his two hands, then points to the surface. He thinks I can make it on one breath?

I look into Sea Boy's eyes. Their gray has a milky sheen underwater, where the surface of the eye seems to reflect the light strangely. He helped me with my leg, and he's learned how long I can go between breaths. I want to trust him.

How poisonous are these things? I point to the jellyfish and make a cutting motion across my throat, questioning with my eyebrows. He nods, eyes wide. He points to the purple mark on his cheek, then copies my mime, adding a face with his eyes shut and tongue out. It seems to be an impression of someone dead.

Great. Quite poisonous, then.

I rise to the surface and breathe extra deeply, emptying my lungs and filling them three times. If I can go a length and a half underwater on one breath in the pool, I can do this. I dive down and circle my arms back around Sea Boy tightly. As soon as I've hooked my feet around his ankles, we stream through the water to the base of the jellyfish mass and curve beneath. The tips of the manta ray's huge wings kick up puffs of sediment from the seabed. My ears pop, and the pressure squeezes my skull. I sense the mass of jellyfish, a whitish thundercloud above us, even though I can't see them at this speed.

My chest is too tight already. With that thought, panic crushes me without warning, and I do the worst thing. I gasp.

Blurting out my air, I lose my grip on Sea Boy's waist. He and the manta ray speed on for a few beats, and I flounder, buffeted in their wake toward the pulsing tentacles above. Sea Boy swims free of the manta ray, circles back, and hauls me down by my waist. My eyes dart frantically. The jellyfish stretch above us in every direction, a toxic ceiling. But the tightness in my chest is now unbearable. I have to breathe.

I meet the boy's eyes through my goggles—his hands grip my waist tight. He's holding me still, moving his lips, his eyes desperate for my understanding—but what is there to understand? I *know* the jellyfish are poisonous, but I also need air or I'll die.

My lungs shudder, and I jerk up my knee, connecting with

his thigh. In a swift movement Sea Boy encircles me from behind, one arm around my shoulders, the other pinning my arms to my sides.

No. His heart thumps against my spine, my chest is bursting. I buck and arch my back, summoning all my strength to jab my elbows into him and kick frantically with my heels.

Let me go!

I throw my head back and pound it against his collarbone. I contort my hands and scratch at any skin I can reach. Black blotches spread across my vision like spilled ink, broken by flashes of light. The urge to breathe is almost overwhelming, but I must get free, get to the surface.

You are drowning me!

Time slows.

The hiss of the oxygen tank. Mom's voice.

Reach.

Kick.

Breathe.

In a burst of strength I jerk both knees up and plunge forward. The boy's arm is within reach of my mouth. Aster is gone, and only animal instinct is left. I chomp my teeth down on Sea Boy's forearm, tearing my head from side to side, flooding my mouth with his molten-metal blood. His hold on me releases a little.

Just enough.

I twist from Sea Boy's grip and kick upward. His hand catches at my ankle and I kick savagely, my heel connecting. As I shoot through the white, pulsating cloud of jellyfish all I can think of is air. I feel the fleshy bodies, the tickle of tentacles brushing past me. No pain. The jellyfish aren't poisonous after all. It's bright, I must be near the surface—

Agony hits. I judder just below the surface, paralyzed and convulsing as the jellyfish stings set the entire surface of my skin aflame.

14

Sam looks up at the sky and pedals harder. His route home from his weekend job at the bike shop takes him along the river path, and the low-slung clouds make it darker than it usually is. Should have brought his bike lights; Granda would have something to say about him not being prepared. He sighs at the thought of Granda. He's still in hospital and doesn't seem to be getting any better.

Sam sees no one on the last kilometer to his house, so when

the figure on the bench in front of him stands and says his name, he skids, almost losing balance, righting himself just in time, his back wheel overhanging the canal by a couple of centimeters.

"Hey, what the—?"

"Sorry, I didn't mean to startle you." The man reaches out as if to help, but then meets Sam's eyes and raises his hands. Sam glares at him, still straddling the crossbar of his bike, feet firmly on the ground.

Sam takes in the broad, open face and blue-green eyes, the eyebrows rising in the center, giving the man a surprised or concerned look. At first Sam thinks it can't actually be him. He's thought about the doctor so much, he's seeing things.

The man steps forward, smiling. "I'm Dr. Nygard; we met briefly at the hospital. You emailed me. I hope you don't mind, but I thought it better we speak in person."

"How did you know I'd be here?" says Sam. He asked to chat to the guy, not for him to stalk him.

"Your grandfather told me where you work. He's incredibly fond of you."

Sam frowns and raises his eyebrows at the same time, and Dr. Nygard continues.

"I understand why you have questions. My association with your grandfather is through a medical trial that unfortunately finished early."

"So why did the trial stop? It seemed to be working for Granda."

"There were—circumstances—beyond my control."

A woman has appeared on the path in the distance. The doctor startled him, but his tone is friendly enough. Sam tries to relax and starts to walk toward home. The doctor strides beside him in silence, and Sam wonders if the guy really doesn't recognize him from the fire site. It's possible, he supposes. He decides to just say it.

"We also met at that fire site in the bush near Tokomaru. I don't know if you remember."

Sam watches the doctor's jaw tighten and his Adam's apple move as he swallows. He feels a flush of adrenaline because whatever the doctor says next, Sam knows for sure now that this is the same man.

"What do you know about the ecovillage, Sam?" Dr. Nygard speaks slowly.

Sam pauses, wondering if the doctor is going to admit he was there.

"Nothing. I just wanted to find out where those girls went."

Dr. Nygard draws a deep breath.

"I remember seeing you, Sam. And I owe you an apology. The camp was private, our work there was sensitive—and I was in shock when we first met, from the fire. You see, I was working with a colleague there, and the people living there were also part of my—our—study. But she wanted less and less contact from the outside world. She's moved to a new location without telling me and took essential research with her. I am concerned about the people who lived there; my colleague's behavior had become . . . erratic."

Sam bites his lip as he remembers the photos. At least the guy doesn't seem to be lying now. So those girls and all the other young people at the camp were part of a medical study? They seemed pretty young and healthy-looking to be ill. The doctor doesn't know he's seen those photos, and Sam decides to keep that information to himself for now, see if whatever else the doctor says adds up.

"So what sort of study were the people at this ecovillage involved in? Were they also on the trial for Marisogen, like Granda?"

Nygard darts a sideways glance at Sam, and he remembers Granda told him a disclaimer meant he wasn't allowed to talk about the trial.

"Not exactly. My colleague was never involved in the Marisogen trial as such, that was my project. It stemmed from our joint research, but I was in charge of the laboratory near the camp. When she left, she took that research and emptied my lab. She even burned down the camp. Her disappearance meant I couldn't continue my work."

Sam remembers the bunker-like building he'd found near the fire site. That must have been the lab.

The doctor slows to a stop, and Sam turns to face him. Creases of concern ripple the guy's forehead, and his eyes are sincere.

"Trust me, Sam," says Dr. Nygard, "the well-being of the camp residents is of critical importance to me. I have spent considerable time searching for them."

Dr. Nygard's eyes remain on his, and Sam holds the eye contact. The doctor's expression is soft, friendly, but there is something fixed about it. Sam opens his mouth to tell him about the phone; it being left at the cove could be linked to the disappearance of everyone in the ecovillage. But something stops him speaking. Disappearing isn't easy, and this colleague of his must have had her reasons to do something so drastic.

"Well, if you ever hear anything, please do contact me, Sam. Any detail you find out, any clue, even the most insignificant thing the girls might have said, could be important. It could mean the continuation of the Marisogen trial and helping a lot of people," he says. "Email me anytime."

"So if you found them, could you pick up Granda's treatment where you left off, or would you need to start your research all over again?"

"With his consent, I'd put your grandfather back on Marisogen without delay. All I need is the information Iona Wright took with her."

Sam blinks. Of course, his colleague is Iona. Aunt Iona. He remembers the girls talking about her. He and Nygard break eye contact and fall into step again for a few paces.

"You know how to contact me, Sam," says the doctor, and with a brush of his hand on Sam's shoulder, he takes the next turn off the path.

Sam jumps on his bike and rides home a lot faster than normal.

Later that evening, Sam paces around his bedroom. He can't decide whether to contact Nygard again, tell him about the phone. The guy told him about the camp, admitted to his initial lie, but the whole situation is just pretty—strange.

He types in a search for Jonathan Nygard and Iona Wright, clicks on the images tab, and scrolls. There. A smiling young man and woman with white lab coats hanging open to reveal jeans underneath.

Geneticist teams up with oncologist to make leap forward in isolating genetic markers for cancer.

Sam peers at the date. Seventeen years ago. He blinks as he pauses on the young woman. She looks similar to the older girl from the plane, Aster.

There are no other hits that link Dr. Nygard and the girls'

aunt, nothing about the camp in the bush, or a treatment trial, or Marisogen. A search for Iona Wright comes up with various articles related to her work as an oncologist in war zones, refugee camps, and slums. Poppy said this was what she did.

There are also some journal articles. Iona also seems to have an interest in—animals.

Animals?

Sam frowns, wondering if this is a different Iona Wright, but he recognizes her from a photo at the top of one of the articles. He skims through. She's written a few articles about the African lungfish, which is able to slow its metabolism into a state of suspended animation and live outside water for up to five years. The fish is basically dead, then comes alive again. Well, who knew? Sam doesn't see what it has to do with curing cancer. Other articles are about the naked mole rat, an ugly-looking critter that can also survive without oxygen and—Sam sits up straighter.

The naked mole rat is famous in the scientific world as one of the only animals that does not seem to suffer from cancer.

He drums his fingers on the desk and then checks the date on the articles.

So Nygard and Iona worked on the genetic markers thing, then came together again after she'd been studying hibernating, cancer-resisting animals.

What were they really doing together at a secret ecovillage

and a hidden lab in the middle of nowhere? Something freaky with animals?

Sam's knee jiggles. He takes a gulp of his Coke, grimacing; it is flat and warm. The only sounds are the faint whir of his laptop fan and the creaks and sighs of the house settling down for the night. Mom and Dad are in bed, and he should be too.

He frowns, then searches for Nygard alone. There's less about him than there is about Iona. He appears on a few staff lists at hospitals. A blog post on a conspiracy website catches Sam's eye.

PREHISTORIC MERMAID HOAX

Jonathan Nygard, a twenty-year-old Norwegian medical student, took a summer job as a scientific research assistant in Svalbard, studying frozen fossils. He reported he had found a rare example of a prehistoric hominid—one of our ancient ancestors—that had been buried in ice for six million years. This would be amazing enough, but Nygard described the fossil's bones as fused at the knee and foot—a tail! He went on to identify fishlike gills between the ribs.

Nygard's doctored slides and scans were so convincing that a group of professors from top paleontology institutes worldwide planned a trip to the Arctic outpost, but luckily for Nygard, they were put off by severe weather, giving the young hoaxer the chance to admit his trickery.

Sam looks up from the screen. When this hoax took place, Nygard was twenty, a medical student. Way before he became a geneticist or met Iona.

Prehistoric mermaids? Sam winds his fingers into his hair, feeling even more confused.

Then he gets lost in a black hole of research about prehuman ancestors. Most theories agree that humans evolved from apes as they adapted to living on the grassy plains of Africa but that there is no definitive evolutionary reason for modern humans to be nearly hairless, have so much fat beneath their skin, or walk upright. There's something called the aquatic ape theory, but in all the research Sam skims through, he sees nothing about tails. Or gills.

Sam's mind spins.

Nygard and Iona, working together on cancer. Something genetic, maybe.

And then . . .

Two orphans stayed at their burned-out ecovillage and disappeared.

And the Marisogen therapy that worked so well on Granda disappeared with them.

PART THREE
SINKING

15

My skin is on fire. I sense sand shifting beneath me, hear the rush of the sea. I'm on the beach. The world rocks crazily, and when I roll onto my side, my stomach heaves. I vomit until I have nothing left. Pain has control of my body, shaking me, and when I try to open my eyes, a different type of darkness closes in. *No.* I hear my voice groan, and my breath hisses through clenched teeth. I curl inward, my hands clawing at my thighs. I want to tear off my skin, anything to make it stop.

Slivers of memory pierce through the pain. The jellyfish. I was stung badly. But I've survived. Deep breath in, and out. I force myself to stop writhing, lie still. Sea Boy. Impossible. He was holding me down.

The burning dulls to a smolder; either I'm getting used to it or lying still makes it a tiny bit better. I try opening my eyes again. A figure lies on the sand a short distance away. Gray suit.

I'm taken back to the first day, waking on the beach. It's like I've been cursed to have a repeating nightmare.

Who is that? *Poppy.*

I rise onto my hands and knees, yelping and gasping at the pain through my grinding teeth, then crawl toward the figure.

Not Poppy—too big, it's a guy. A curl of reddish hair. Callum. As I crawl faster, the pain gets worse and I'm racked with shivers so bad I can barely hold my weight on my arms.

I stop a meter from Callum.

The front of his gray suit is soaked with something. A dark, wet stain covers the top of his chest. My breaths are loud, catching, filling my head.

My eyes track up to his neck as the dark closes in. I don't want to see but can't stop looking.

Smears of red.

Everything turns to black.

• • •

Darkness. A whisper. "Aster? Can you hear me?"

Then much louder, hurting my ears, "Iona! Iona, she's waking up!"

I blink my eyes open and groan. Iona? I sink back down, half smiling, half sobbing in relief. A dream. A nightmare. Iona's here, so I'm back at the Wildhaven camp . . .

Callum. It didn't happen.

But my skin, it's *prickly*, as if stretched too tight over my bones.

I push myself up on my elbows. The walls are green bamboo poles and the air is warm. The sound of the sea fills my head, and Beti is at the door in bright sunlight, her hair pushed back from her face with a band of woven leaves.

Everything floods back. Sea Boy. The jellyfish. I was stung.

Callum. Not that—that part can't be real.

Beti was calling for Iona. Are the others here?

"Poppy?" I say, my voice cracking.

I swing my legs over the edge of the hammock but remain sitting in it, shaking. A figure runs straight past Beti, and something in the way she moves makes me think for a split second that she's Mom. But it's Iona.

"Where's Poppy?" I say, my tongue thick.

"Shhh, it's OK. It's most likely they are on the other island, on the west side of the atoll. How are you feeling?" she says, her hand on my wrist.

"Where's Callum? Where's Poppy?" I push her away.

"The other island. It's OK. Let's get you some—"

"Tell me!"

Iona kneels on the sand in front of my hammock.

"I'm sorry, Aster. Callum is dead."

"And Poppy?"

"On the other island."

I close my eyes. What I saw was real. I hate myself because through my horror I feel a hit of relief. Callum, not Poppy.

But Callum.

"I saw him, I saw . . ." I whisper.

Beti is standing at the door of the hut, sobs shaking her whole body. Iona stands, folds Beti under her arm, and brings her forward, tears filling her own eyes.

"Callum washed up around the same time you did. He'd suffered—severe chest injuries."

An image of the dark stain on his suit and the red against his skin swims into my mind, and I pitch forward, retching.

I thought I saw something in the sea from the small island, and later by the jellyfish—it could have been him.

"How?"

Beti draws a ragged breath. "He swam off, after you. I couldn't . . . stop him."

Was he hurt by the jellyfish? By Sea Boy? I can't take this in. I can't think. I cover my mouth, swept with nausea.

Iona hands me a drilled coconut and I take a sip. It settles my stomach a little.

"I'm so sorry. We'll get to Poppy and the others soon, I swear to you. They'll be on Halo West," she says, pointing toward the left end of the beach. "Our equipment was programmed to get us to the nearest land, but the sea was rough. We four were the last, and I think that's why we were separated from the others. I was washed up on the opposite side of this island, and it took some time to make my way over here."

I hold my head between my hands, and the hammock rocks as I try to process this. Halo West? The island beyond the mangrove island?

Callum's dead, but Iona's here, and she says Poppy's safe. I start shaking, and my teeth chatter. *Poppy's safe.*

Then Iona's arms wrap around me, and I press my forehead against her warm neck as tears squash from the corners of my eyes. I allow Iona to hold me for a moment and when I push her away, she wipes tears from her own cheeks too. She helps me stand.

"So you were on the other side of this island? How do you know the others aren't there too?" I say.

"I was expecting us all to be on Halo West to start with. I prepared both islands but left extra supplies on West. How are you feeling now?" Iona's eyes never leave my face. I lean on her heavily as I stagger to the door of the hut.

"There was a shark, a boy," I say. "I was . . . stung."

Beti is now outside the hut, sweeping leaves off the sand with a homemade broom. She blinks, her eyes swollen and puffy.

"I'm glad you are OK," says Beti, her voice hitching on a sob. I step over to her and hold her tight, and my stings smart but I barely feel them. I remember the soft lilt of Callum's voice. His relief when Beti woke up, his determination to prove himself, his gruff kindness when he brought me food that first night. Exploring the lagoon with me, the scars on his arms. He can't just be gone.

When Beti and I break apart, Iona leads me to a low makeshift table made from bamboo poles bound together with twine. We sit on the sand. I scan around the camp; the sun is high above. They've added this table, and the firepit is now rimmed with a double row of rocks. How long have I been out?

"I think the poison must have all been metabolized. The swelling is down, and your heart rate was back to normal a couple of hours ago. You aren't in too much pain now?"

"Not pain. Just tender, itchy," I say. I look down at my thighs. They look like a child has scribbled on my skin with a thick purple marker. One arm is the same. I raise my hand to touch my cheek; smooth, but the other side has raised lines, and my lip feels swollen.

"None of the sting sites seem infected," says Iona. "I think they'll heal fine."

I remember Sea Boy's face underwater, the purple scar across his forehead and cheek.

Iona asks about the jellyfish, and I describe them to her.

Beti pushes half a large leaf toward me, then starts sweeping the sand again. I tentatively eat the chunks of mango and peeled shrimps, and they taste so good; my mind is clearing with the energy from the food.

There's a crease of concern between Iona's eyes. "Can you remember what happened?"

When I look at her, I *do* remember: the boat, the gas in the cabin, the locked door.

"What did you— You gassed us? Why?"

Iona crushes her fingers together so hard her knuckles pale.

"Wildhaven was no longer safe. I had to get you out of there."

The food is now tasteless, and I swallow with difficulty, my eyes fastened to her face.

"Wildhaven was a refuge—you know that much." She looks at Beti, who nods. "After many years as an oncologist I became fascinated by more experimental cancer research. I made a discovery, a way to transfer genes from animals who don't suffer from cancer to humans. I contacted an old colleague of mine. Jonathan Nygard was a brilliant geneticist, and we developed a therapy. Years went by, we kept testing it, and in the lab, it worked. But there was no way a therapy of this kind would be licensed. It wouldn't even make it to human trials for decades, maybe never. But I knew it worked!"

Iona's eyes shine.

"I could stop so many people dying like my mother and father had died, like my sister. So I cut my ties and built the Wildhaven camp. Nygard set up a small private lab facility in the forest close by. I offered sanctuary to young people who—in the most basic terms—had genes that tested positive for cancer. I administered my preventative therapy."

My eyes don't leave her face. What she is saying matches up with what Beti and Callum told me, but it's a whole different thing hearing it directly from Iona. She's proud. Proud of what she's done here.

"Your mom agreed to have you and Poppy tested for genetic markers years ago. The fever you experienced at Wildhaven was the therapy integrating into your body through a carrier virus."

I notice the creases around her eyes seem deeper. My relief at seeing her is evaporating as she speaks. Because in any reality—even with the best intentions and their consent—she treated vulnerable teenagers with an untested drug. And that's before we even get on to what happened on the boat or sweeping us away to this island.

I press my lips together as she continues.

"But Jonathan Nygard had his own agenda, and I still don't know what it was. The next part of the therapy plan was to live a healthy, basic lifestyle until a few years had passed and we could test again. If we were mostly self-sufficient there was no way for us to be discovered. But Nygard was determined to continue with unnecessary blood tests. The tests showed nothing new; we needed to give it time before we even considered how to share our findings. But he was impatient, obsessed, and wouldn't explain his insistence on the continued sampling. I'd promised to provide a true haven for these young people, and we'd become a family. It was becoming impossible to work with him, but I realized it would be relatively easy for Nygard to sever all links with the project, as I had recruited each and every one of you. If he exposed us, you'd be split up and I would be imprisoned."

Beti clears the table of the remains of my food. She hasn't stopped moving.

"So I trained my students in boatbuilding and island survival. I bought what I needed and prepared. I researched uninhabited islands extensively, found this atoll in the South Pacific—perfect if Wildhaven became unsafe—and managed to make a trip out here. The day you and Poppy arrived, I had already asked Nygard to leave Wildhaven, yet there he was again. The research was ours, but the running of Wildhaven and welfare of the candidates was my responsibility. He didn't need to be there anymore.

"I went to the lab the day after you arrived and found Nygard had collected vast banks of blood samples I knew nothing about. The lab was always his domain, and the camp was mine, but I should have watched him more carefully. He'd been taking extra during routine checks for months. I destroyed them all, cleared the lab. I was now sure Nygard wanted to *use* your samples for something. He needed more, and he was going to find a way to get more. I had to get you to the atoll cleanly, quickly, before he could suspect anything. So I used the gas on the boat, and you were dropped into the sea. I'm sorry it was so—distressing."

"I thought you were killing us," I blurt out, the harshness in my voice taking me by surprise. "Why didn't you *tell* us what you were doing, that we needed to get away from him?"

"Because if even one of you refused to leave, the whole project would be at risk."

It's so insane, I don't even know what to say next.

"So you discovered a cancer vaccine therapy and you used it on us, then destroyed it?" I say, becoming more confused by the second.

"Oh no. I have backed up all my research. I will go back to it, once enough time has passed to be sure of results."

"So we might still get cancer?" I say.

"The chances are infinitesimal. But to have any credibility, the study needs time."

I grind my teeth. My aunt is ill. She's suffering from a psychological illness, some sort of God complex. I press my thumb into the skin between the thumb and forefinger of my opposite hand until it hurts. I need to focus. She said she could get me to Poppy.

"And you did all this by yourself?" says Beti.

"Before we left Wildhaven I shared what was going to happen with a few of the oldest students, who helped."

Beti stops sweeping and stares at the ground.

"So why not simply sail to the island in the boat? Why the crazy life jackets?" I say.

Iona nods. "Nygard was away on business for a week, but I knew he would come looking for us the moment he found out we were gone. The boat would have been detectable by plane. Jonathan is a very clever man, and I had to be sure we weren't followed, so I sailed to the island and sank the boat. I'd commissioned the lifesaver jackets at the same time I found the island; they were prototypes with motors and sensing systems to tow you to shallow waters. I rigged you to life support and released you, unconscious. You'd be impossible to trace that way."

I look down at the marks on the insides of my wrists from the tubes, already scabbed over. Life support.

I stare at Iona. I was mistaken in ever thinking she was anything like my mom.

"So you planned for everyone to live here. How long for?" I say.

Iona raises one shoulder. "The atoll should be able to support us indefinitely. But I'd been thinking we could stay here for two, maybe three years."

"And if we want to leave, we'll have to build a boat from what we have here?"

Iona nods.

I look down at the jellyfish stings across the backs of my hands. When I straighten my fingers, it tingles like sunburn and I remember the pain, my silent screams into the sea. I thought I was dying. For the second time.

We're in the South Pacific, possibly thousands of miles from anywhere, no phones, no civilization. This atoll is her little cancer-free Eden.

"Poppy and I did not consent to any of this," I say, my voice rising again.

Iona pauses. "I didn't have time to explain everything to you with the way Jonathan was behaving," she says, then meets my eyes. "But I knew it was what your mom would have wanted."

My nails gouge into my palms. I want to scream at her, to lash out. She has no idea what Mom wanted—she wasn't even there at the end. Another realization strikes me hard, cranking my heart rate and snatching my breath.

"If you had this cure, this therapy, then why didn't you treat Mom?" I say.

"The genes can only integrate into the cells *before* the cancer has taken hold. We haven't begun developing a treatment for existing sufferers, but it was going to be our next step. I believe it can be done one day."

I breathe through my nose. Bring the focus back to Poppy.

"You can definitely get us to the others, to Poppy?" I say quietly. I hold my aunt's gaze, her deep-set eyes, so like my little sister's.

Iona lowers her chin, and her mouth forms a determined line. "It's my absolute priority."

We nod at each other, then I look away.

"Are you ready to tell us what happened to you?" says Iona, gently.

I recall the indentations across the boy's chest, behind his ears, opening to breathe seawater. I look out at the lagoon and wish they could see him for themselves. I remember swimming to the mangrove island, cutting my knee, the shark.

Sea Boy.

I take a deep breath.

16

". . . and the boy . . . he could breathe underwater. Through gills." I catch Iona's and Beti's expressions. I'm babbling now, but I can't stop. "He couldn't talk, couldn't breathe on land. He bandaged my knee with seaweed stuff. He rode a . . . a manta ray . . ."

I falter. It sounds ridiculous. Iona slowly nods.

"The sting toxin had a strong hallucinogenic effect. Combined with the shock of what you've seen . . ."

Iona doesn't believe me.

"The boy wasn't a hallucination! He swam with his feet together, a dolphin kick, and he wore rags but had spears and knives. I met him way before I even saw a jellyfish, before I was stung," I say, my words garbling together. The heat in my cheeks travels to my chest as I imagine how I must sound.

Sea Boy held me down beneath the jellyfish. If I hadn't escaped him, I would have drowned. But I suspect he got me back to the island somehow, because how did I get back otherwise?

Did he bring Callum back too? Could he have had something to do with his death?

"Jellyfish toxins are agonizing. Extreme pain can cause a break from reality, a state of delirium. Plus you've been under incredible stress, were dehydrated, possibly suffering from exposure—"

I release a barking laugh as I remember thinking the same things myself when I saw the boy's impossible face through the water. I force my voice to be calm although I feel panic rising.

"You have to believe me. Look," I say, lifting my knee. The cut is sealed, and there's no sign of how deep it was, or of the sticky seaweed. The mark is almost lost in the scrawled purple stings all around it.

Iona meets my eyes, and her sympathetic look makes my heart thump against my ribs.

She's making it seem like *I'm* crazy? She's the one who experimented on us, who knocked us unconscious and brought us to the middle of nowhere. And now Callum is dead. If Callum can be dead, then Poppy—

Don't think it.

I pull down the neck of my swimsuit. "The boy's gills were here," I say, tracing a shaking finger between my ribs, then behind my ears. "I saw them up close, I know I did."

Iona tries to take my hand, but I snatch it away.

"Aster—it seems likely that you and Callum were together when he was attacked, as his injuries were in the places you describe. One way for the brain to process a traumatic incident is to frame it in a fantastical way. His injuries were unusual, possibly made by a clawed animal. When you start to remember—"

"I *do* remember. We weren't together, I told you what happened. I know where his injuries were"—my voice hisses between my teeth—"because I saw him on the beach."

I stare at Iona, then close my mouth. "I want to see him now."

"You were unconscious through the whole evening and night and most of today. We've already buried him, Aster," says Iona.

I stand abruptly and sway, light-headed. This is my fault. I should have listened to Poppy. Why couldn't I see there was something wrong about that camp, about what Iona was doing? I remember the glove I found in the crevice on the mangrove island and check my waist. I'm not even wearing the belt. I'm in the beige shorts and T-shirt from the first day.

"I found a glove—on the small island . . ." I trail off. Is there any chance she could be right, that I hallucinated all this?

Iona shakes her head. "I haven't seen a glove, Aster. I'm sorry."

She really does look sorry. Sorry for me. I can't trust her, so I can't trust Poppy is safe.

My breath hitches in my throat. The hissing sound fills my ears. The beach blurs, but a bright rim of light glows around Iona.

The urge to escape overwhelms me. This is the panic coming, but even as I recognize it, I can't control it. There is nowhere to go. I want home. I need my mom.

Fear descends too fast. My heart pounds in my ears and against my skull.

I lean over with my hands on my thighs, counting out loud through numb lips. I can't get enough air in through my nose. Iona is talking, but I can't hear her. I stagger back, knocking into the table. My desperation to prevent the panic attack brings it on more quickly. Paralyzing, unfocused fear mounts with the inevitability of water building against a bulging dam. My palms are slippery with sweat.

All sound fades, replaced by an oxygen tank hiss inside my head.

Mom. The hospital. The hiss. I need it to stop, but I know what it means when it does.

Not enough . . . air. Every muscle trembles.

I have to find shelter. Dark. I give in to the flight response, and I sprint.

The sand flicking up behind me hits the back of my legs, and I'm overwhelmed by the terror that someone is chasing me down.

My field of vision narrows, my throat closes. I can't breathe. I'm dying. This is how my full panic attacks feel—I know that—but I can't convince myself that I've been through this before and survived. This time feels different, worse. I tell myself it *always* feels worse, but there's a vicious war raging in my mind, and reasonable thought is collateral damage.

I slam into the rocks at the west end of the beach and collapse against them, gasping. The world spins, and bile burns the back of my throat. I find a crevice and squash into it, rolling myself into a ball, rocking back and forth in the tiny amount of space it allows me. I press my fingers to my lips, but there's no feeling there. My heart batters my rib cage, struggling, jumping. My body is failing me. I'm not dying, yet the larger part of me believes I am. The noise in my ears rises to a scream, but over it I hear a voice.

"Aster, listen to me. Concentrate on my voice."

I try to focus on the sound, vaguely aware I am whimpering.

"Look around you, touch the rock, listen to the sea."

I do as Iona says, running my hypersensitive fingertips over the rough boulder. It brings me back enough that I can start to count my breaths. Three in. Six out.

The noise in my head fades. My senses are so heightened that I hear Iona's lips moving as she counts with me. Sensation tingles into my own lips again. Like a cat that has finished toying with a mouse, the fear releases me, and I become aware of my surroundings. I'm jammed into a crevice like a cornered fox. A cold, damp blanket of shame settles over me. Callum is dead because he swam after me. This place isn't safe; I have to get to Poppy. They won't believe me about Sea Boy. Why would they?

"I'll give you some space."

The sand scrunches beneath Iona's bare feet as she walks away.

I shiver in the aftermath of the adrenaline, a metallic taste in my mouth. I'm a wreck of what I used to be. A liability with my paranoia, anxiety, and panic attacks. I can't even think about my mom. Maybe Poppy is better off on the other island without me.

The last time I spoke to Callum he was sitting on the cool sand in the moonlight. He had hinted that he'd follow Iona anywhere, but in reality, he had no one else and nowhere else to go.

Iona might have gotten consent from the others, but Iona didn't give any of us a real choice.

That thought reignites my anger and jerks me out of self-pity.

I'm all Poppy's got, and this place might look beautiful, but it is dangerous, deadly. We are both here because I didn't listen to my sister, and I will not let her down again.

17

Sam finishes his lunch break and unlocks the door to the mountain bike shop. He's picked up some extra shifts during the holidays and has been left alone for a few hours while his boss runs some errands. Tuesday is a quiet day, and he's spent most of the morning watching reviews of the latest bikes on his laptop. He enters the shop and stops still. It looks just as he left it: bikes lined up along the front window, accessories on wall brackets, everything in its place. Yet something is different. A breath of breeze touches his face although the front door is closed behind him. The door to the stockroom sways. Did he leave the back door open? It only leads to a tiny yard containing the bins—his boss keeps it locked, and the keys are in the register.

Sam's muscles tense, and an electric feeling passes over his skin.

"Jake?" He calls his boss's name, not liking the quaver in his voice. No answer. The stockroom door swings again.

If there's someone out there, Sam knows he should leave and call the police. He grips the phone in his jeans pocket and strides over to the till, eyes still on the door. Jake could have forgotten to close the back door earlier. No big deal—in a minute he will laugh about how jumpy he got over nothing.

The register is closed, as he left it.

Gripping his phone like a lifeline, Sam pushes open the door to the stockroom and switches on the light quickly, like he did when he woke up as a kid, scared of the dark. The white glow from the fluorescent strip floods the room. Sam sighs. The back door is swinging.

This isn't right.

Sam looks closer. There's a large gouge in the wood next to the lock. The doorframe is splintered. Someone *was* in here.

Sam spins around. There's no one here now. Everything looks the same as when he tidied it before lunch. They could still be out the back. Prickles travel down his neck; he wants to run. He grabs a wrench.

"Hello?" he says.

What is he doing? Greeting the burglar? He knows he should run straight out the front of the shop, but he grips the cold metal of the wrench and steps forward to the damaged back door. He kicks it wide open, hurting his toe through his Converse. The door slams against the wall. He waits. Trembling. Nothing. He peers around the door. Nothing in the yard. Bins, cardboard.

"They're gone. They're gone," he whispers to himself, his heart rate slowing.

Sam's hands shake as he surveys the splintered door and doorframe.

He calls Jake. Leaves a message, babbling, not really aware of what he is saying. He calls 911 and asks for the police. When they assure him someone is on their way, he surveys the stockroom. There really is no evidence anyone has been in here, nothing stolen, nothing knocked off the racks. He turns back to the door. It doesn't look like they even attempted to pick the lock, simply levered it open with a tool, cracking both the door and the frame open.

Sam imagines the force, determination, and planning required to do that and feels sick. He walks back into the shop, and as he passes the counter he stops. His laptop was under there.

Sam knows before he looks. His laptop, stowed on the narrow shelf under the counter, out of sight, is gone. He runs his hand beneath the counter and checks the drawers, although he knows exactly where he left it.

Sam's laptop is the only thing that has been taken.

The police say the break-in seems professional, even though there were thousands of dollars' worth of bikes ripe for the picking and they took only his old laptop.

Whoever did it only wanted that one item. They had *targeted* Sam.

Nygard must have sensed Sam was holding something back. He was desperate to find the people from the camp.

Was he *that* desperate?

But who else could it be? If this was Nygard, he'll see Sam's browsing history and know Sam's been researching him. Sam took out the girl's memory card and left it at home. Nygard won't know he has the photos or the phone.

The doctor didn't seem like the type to do something like this, but if those kids were in danger and he really had lost the research for a cancer cure, then Sam guessed that would be reason enough to steal a laptop. He hadn't hurt anyone, hadn't even caused much damage.

Sam waits outside the shop as the police officer finishes dusting for fingerprints.

He could never tell the police about Nygard, Iona Wright, the girls, the camp, and he can't accuse Nygard directly. It would sound paranoid and crazy, since he has no real evidence . . .

He desperately wants to speak to Granda. Sam is about to call his cell phone but sees four missed calls from his mom, so he calls her instead. She doesn't answer right away.

Mom answers. "Sam, thank goodness. Don't panic, but Granda is in the intensive care unit. We're at the hospital."

18

I walk along the shallows of the lagoon, paddling my feet, scooping up water to splash on my arms and cool off. This morning's work on the sailing canoe was intense; we had to drag the last of the timbers we need from inland, and my back and legs ache.

We started working on the sailing canoe right away, the night after my panic attack. In the last few days we've collected all the timber we need, and the skeleton of the craft is built.

I avoid meeting Iona's eyes and speak to her only when I have to. I blame myself for Callum, but she's to blame for this whole mess. It's awkward because we need to make the boat together, live in this deserted place together. So I tell myself to be quiet, don't think, try not to feel, do the work, find Poppy.

I haven't mentioned Sea Boy again to either Iona or Beti. I need to *prove* to them that he is real. Because—I can't even get my head around it. I felt like he wanted to help me, but then underneath the jellyfish he tried pretty hard to drown me. And then there's Callum and the mystery of what killed him. Could Sea Boy have done that to him? I can't make myself believe that. Sometimes I imagine Sea Boy as friendly; he could swim to the other island, see if Poppy is there, maybe even take me there on his manta ray. It sounds crazy even thinking it, but I know it is possible. And if he isn't friendly, then Iona and Beti should know.

I fix the image of his chest in my mind, the fine furrows of his gills falling between his ribs. I'd never hallucinate something so precise, so realistic. Would I?

What Iona said—that it's a way to cope with Callum's death—can't be true. The wounds on his chest and neck must have been a coincidence. It's hard to think of Callum. I didn't really know him, so I don't know if what I'm feeling is real grief. The strangled anger I feel when I think of him is real though. He'd already been through enough. He trusted in Iona's treatment, her haven. But he swam after me, to help *me.* Beti starts down the sand toward me, and I stop walking and wait for her. She holds up two snorkels and in her other hand shows me a couple of nose clips.

"Where did you get those?" I say.

"Bottom of the back pocket of the life jacket. Iona showed me," says Beti. She raises her eyebrows in a question, nodding toward the lagoon. Her eyes are red-rimmed. Callum.

My skin is still healing from the stings and feels tight in the sun's glare. The water would be cooling, but the last time I swam was beneath the jellyfish, terrified my lungs were about to fill with water. I haven't swum properly since.

I shake my head. "Sorry, Beti, I can't. Not yet."

"We're stuck on a tropical island, in case you hadn't noticed," she says, pointing around us. "You can't avoid the sea forever."

I feel a burn of anger; she's asking too much from me. But my shoulders slump, because she's right.

I wade in and find the salt doesn't hurt my stings; the lagoon is warm, but cooler than my hot skin, and soothing. I position the nose clip, adjust the goggles, and bite down on the rubber of the snorkel. Beti does the same and then grins around the mouthpiece and says "ready" in a garbled voice through the snorkel tube. I find myself smiling despite my sadness.

I give her the OK sign, and we push off into the turquoise water.

The first day we arrived I couldn't appreciate the lagoon properly. It really is beautiful. I remember how to hold my breath when diving under with the snorkel and then blow out the water when I surface. After Beti has a coughing fit, I show her and she gets the hang of it too. As I swim, I scan around and realize that rather than looking for Poppy, I'm checking for Sea Boy. My gut tells me he won't appear now, but I'm also sure he was the shadow I saw through the gap in the reef on the first day. He is curious about us—that was clear from the way he behaved.

I've always been able to think more clearly in the water. I feel calm and grateful to Beti.

We explore the corals, and a huge shoal of striped yellow and silvery-blue fish encloses us for a moment before swimming on alongside the reef. They stop and start to peck at the coral, making loud ticking sounds. I remember Poppy's glee when she found out fish that ate coral pooped sand. When the fish disperse, I see something larger in the blue distance ahead. Beti grips my arm, and I remember the shark. Would it come into the lagoon? We both freeze, then the shape materializes into a turtle. It sweeps directly toward us and seems to give us a beady glare, only swerving at the last moment as it heads through the gap in the reef beyond us.

Beti and I surface and spit out the snorkels as we tread water. The lagoon is around three meters deep at this end. "Did you see the look on his face?" she says. "Like he was annoyed we were in his way."

I nod. "It's really beautiful here."

I meet Beti's eyes and have to look away, my chest tight. Her eyes are full of Callum, and the girl with me here should be Poppy. *Please let her be safe.* I dive back under.

At the far end of the lagoon is a meadow of waving seagrass, and we swim toward it. I hold out a hand, and the fronds tickle my fingers. I catch a glimpse of almost luminous yellow and dive down to get a closer look. I part the grass and reveal a family of tiny bright yellow seahorses, their curling tails wound around the blades of seagrass. I beckon to Beti above, and when I turn back, one of the tiniest seahorses has lost hold of its anchor and is floating away from its family in the slight current. When I scoop the water around the tiny creature, it twirls its tail around my little finger. It is so delicate and so very bright, it doesn't seem real. I'm running out of breath. I gently detach it and guide it back the others, where it finds a frond to grip on to. I take one last glance at the miniature family before swimming back to the surface.

I feel ready to go back to camp. I indicate that to Beti beneath the surface, and we turn for shore. Then I spot something on the seabed, at the deepest part of the lagoon. A raised pattern in the sand about two meters across, an intricate design of concentric circles made from peaks and troughs.

I rise to the surface, being careful not to damage the delicate structure beneath us with the turbulence from my feet.

I shrug at Beti, but it's clear she doesn't know what it is either.

Back at the camp, Beti tells Iona about the turtle and the fish we saw.

"How are your stings feeling?" says Iona to me.

"Better," I say. We are all acting a part, dodging the big hole in the center of camp where Callum should be, where Iona gassed us and lost my little sister.

I feel calmer after my swim. Being reliant on Iona to get us to Poppy makes me so angry, but it's an emotion I can't afford.

I slip back into the same sawdust-stained shorts and T-shirt. Iona has explained that there are more supplies on Halo West Island—clothes, medical equipment—in a trunk she set up some time ago. She told us how she found the atoll on maps of the South Pacific, how it was once in a nuclear testing zone that had never been used and was now decommissioned, far away from shipping lanes.

Iona gathers more firewood, and Beti suggests we collect water.

The water carriers are cylinders of foil-like material that roll up really small. I'm struck again by how carefully Iona prepared for all this. We take one each.

Beti chats as we walk, telling me about a new fruit bush

she's found. We already have mangoes, pineapple, and giant grapefruit things called pomelos.

"Iona says we need to start rationing the fruit as the trees are so young. So I hope you like coconut and fish," she says, crouching to fill the water pouch in the stream, up where it flows over rocks at the tree line.

"Luckily," I say.

"And seaweed?" she says.

"Around the outside of sushi? Then yes," I say, copying her as I fill my pouch with water.

Beti stops. "That is exactly what Callum said."

"I'm sorry," I say without looking at her. Callum was Beti's friend, part of her family at Wildhaven. I've wanted to say this but haven't found the words until now. "It's my fault. He went in after me."

"I told him not to go," she says. "It was his choice. Sad thing was, he always wanted to prove that he was useful, strong. But he didn't need to change. Everyone liked him as he was."

We fall into stride.

On the way back, Beti describes how on the other island, there will be equipment to set up something called mariculture: an underwater farm with baskets suspended from ropes for growing shellfish, like the one I saw on the beach back in New Zealand.

"Don't you ever miss normal stuff?" I say. "I mean, you're used to it now, but when you first came to Wildhaven."

As the words leave my mouth, I remember that before Wildhaven, Beti was living in a refugee camp with her dying mother. I feel embarrassed by my insensitivity, but Beti doesn't seem to notice.

"Not really," she says. "I missed music at first, but nothing from before seems that important to me now. Do you?"

I miss my phone and music, my hairdryer. Toast and Marmite. I would give my right arm for a can of cold Coke or a fluffy towel. But none of it matters, not really, not compared to how much I miss Mom and now Poppy, every day.

"Just my family," I say.

She gives me a rueful smile and nods, then slips her arm through mine, and we walk on.

Later we share a meal at the makeshift table, the fire warm at my back.

Beti asks Iona about the design we saw in the sand on the seabed, demonstrating how large it was by walking a circle around the fire.

"I'd have to see it, but it sounds like a puffer fish nest. They are made by fish about this big," says Iona, holding her hands about ten centimeters apart.

"But it was so detailed," says Beti. "How was it made by one little fish?"

"The puffer fish builds it bit by tiny bit and eventually creates something unique—miraculous, really."

Iona stares intently into the flames.

"Are there any animals here on the island? I haven't seen any," says Beti.

I decide it's time I prove to Iona that I'm fine. I don't want her watching my every move, sending Beti to supervise me. I can trust myself to keep calm now, and I need to talk.

"An atoll is the remains of a sea volcano, the volcano has sunk down, and the ring of islands is the ancient reef that formed around it. It was never joined to other land. So unless humans brought them, the only animals would have come by wind, water, or flying here from the mainland," I say.

Iona grins. "A scientist after my own heart! I couldn't have said it better. And we are so far from the mainland, there is very little here. Probably not even birds."

Yet there is a boy underwater. Sea Boy seems more unreal by the second.

Beti is staring at me, open-mouthed. "How do you know this?" she says.

"I liked science at school," I say with a shrug.

"Are there sandflies?" says Beti.

This time Iona and I start speaking at the same time: "Not without any mammals . . ."

We break off, and Iona smiles at me. I manage a small smile back.

Beti wrinkles her nose. "This is good news," she says, and I wonder if she means Iona and me talking to each other or the lack of biting insects. "At Wildhaven they even ate my eyelids."

We laugh, but it's a hollow sound. Three of us. So different from the bustle at Wildhaven. I imagine Poppy with all the others, surrounded by chat, maybe under a larger shelter like the one in the center of Wildhaven. She's a lot better at making friends than I am. She'll be safe until I get to her. I force myself to believe it.

By the time we climb into our hammocks, I've decided I have to go back to the lagoon alone. To the gap in the reef, to see if I can somehow signal to Sea Boy. He could be dangerous, but I have to know if he's real.

I tell myself that if he wanted to kill me, he'd have already done it.

I sleep with my swimsuit on beneath my T-shirt, certain I'll wake before dawn; I always do.

19

I wake earlier than ever and watch for the first hint of the sky becoming lighter through the gaps in the bamboo hut before I tip silently out of the hammock and edge open the door. I turn and check Iona and Beti; their breathing is heavy and rhythmic. Six a.m. swim training made me a master at sneaking out without waking Mom and Poppy. Mom never liked it; she preferred to hear me leave, but she worked long shifts as a nurse and didn't need to wake extra early just to see me off. I feel a blast of familiar fury. She was sick to gone so quickly.

This morning I'm locking my fear for Poppy and my grief for Mom in the darkest part of my heart. I need to concentrate on the here and now.

Sea Boy held me down beneath the jellyfish. But I tell myself again that if he had actually intended to kill me, he could so easily have done it then, or earlier, with his knife or his spear or simply by leaving me on the mangrove island with the choice of thirst or shark.

So with the dawn breeze in my hair and cool sand beneath my toes, I set off to look for the boy who either tried to drown me or to save my life. To see what he knows about Callum, if he has seen Poppy. To find out if I can trust my own eyes and mind.

I lift my chin. I don't know how I am going to signal to him, and I feel exposed in only my swimsuit. I'm choosing to believe he didn't want to kill me, but being armed seems a good idea. I already have my knife, and I tiptoe toward the tree line, retrieving my machete from where I hid it last night. I attach it to my belt.

I half jog down the beach, all the while expecting Iona to notice I'm gone and call out. But she doesn't.

I hesitate at the water's edge. Last time I went off on my own, I swam to the mangrove island and Callum followed me—and died. But I need to do this. This time I'm armed, and I don't intend to leave the lagoon. This is a calculated risk. I slide into the lagoon, surprised at how warm the water is. Clouds build like silver-topped mountains along the horizon. For now the moon is brighter than the blue smudge of sunrise and penetrates the water with rays of gunmetal gray. I lower the goggles, clasp on the nose clip, and bite down on the snorkel.

The lagoon is dark, eerie. Fewer fish around, but other things move on the reef. An eel darts in and out of a hollow, and I catch sight of a sleek body that looks shark-shaped but is only the length of my arm.

I shudder, strike out toward the gap in the reef, and then dive and hover at the brink of the murkier water beyond. I stare around me through the goggles as goose bumps rise along my arms.

Reach. Kick. Breathe.

I tell my mom's voice that now is not a good time.

There's nothing. The darkness below and beyond is limitless, bewildering.

The sound of my breath through the snorkel tube breaks the silence, and I take a deep inhalation and hold it. I hear a ticking sound and look down to see one lone fish pecking at the coral.

Sea Boy made a noise with his teeth to call the manta ray, a clicking sound that traveled through the water. I open my jaw, ready to try it. But what if the clicking calls a manta ray? I don't know if I want one of those giant fish sweeping up to me.

What else could make a noise that will carry?

I draw my knife and machete and rap the metal blades together as hard as I can against the resistance of the water.

I take a deep breath through the snorkel and hold it again, listening. I make the noise again, over and over. It's useless. Sea Boy could travel miles on that giant fish—he could be anywhere in the entire ocean.

Or buried back within my hallucinating subconscious where he belongs.

I turn and kick back into the safety of the lagoon. Swimming slowly toward the beach, I pause above the circular design in the sand that Iona said was made by a single puffer fish.

I take a breath and dive down. It somehow looks even more impressive and detailed in the heavy shadows of the dim light. And then I spot the creator. A boxy, spotted fish with wide-spaced eyes swims along the troughs, his body tilted sideways so he can plow the circular shape with a tiny vibrating fin. I remember the faraway look in Iona's eyes as she told us about this fish. It occurs to me that Wildhaven, her cure, getting us to this atoll, is Iona's pattern in the sand—impossible to believe, but here all the same. And yet I could wreck this fish's heroic work with just one sweep of my foot. I shiver, then surface and turn back to the gap in the reef.

One last try at calling Sea Boy. One last shot of faith in my own eyes, my own sanity.

I tap the machete and knife together over and over. The staccato, metallic beats echo across the ocean, and I feel like I'm shouting in a church, but I carry on even when my arms ache.

A mass streams beneath me, and before I can move, it swoops up in front and I spin in Sea Boy's wake, my heart beating in my throat. He grasps my forearm to hold me still and faces me, his eyebrows arched. The bioluminescent globes attached to his shoulders flicker violet-blue, clearer now in the darker water. They illuminate his face from below as the predawn light dapples him from above. He seems carved from marble.

Sea Boy *is* real.

What was I thinking summoning him here?

Now that we're face-to-face, the fact he tried to drown me feels *very* important.

I shake myself free of his grip and flail backward, breathing raggedly through the snorkel, realizing my self-doubt had grown so big, I hadn't believed Sea Boy existed, let alone that I would be able to call him to the lagoon.

I hold out both the machete and knife like a little kid who wants to play swords. His gills are slim lines across his chest, and his dark hair billows. He surveys me over the top of my weapons, one eyebrow raised. He's holding a black spine like the ones from those spiky sea urchins. With the other hand he points to my arms and legs and makes a wriggling movement with his fingers followed by the same cutting gesture across his neck that he made when we first saw the jellyfish.

My heart races. I don't know what he's trying to say, can't make out his expression. Something about the jellyfish?

Slowing my juddering breaths through the snorkel, I give an exaggerated shrug.

I need to keep him here, find a way to show Iona and Beti that he's real.

I need to find out more about him, about Callum, about Poppy and the others.

Or I need to escape now before he makes a second attempt at drowning me.

My eyes flick to his wrist. It is wrapped in the same seaweed he used on my leg. I bit him. Hard.

What's *his* reason for coming back? I kick gently, still holding up the knife and machete, trying to drift backward and increase the distance between us.

I need to talk to Sea Boy like I did on the mangrove island, so I point to the surface and raise my eyebrows. The first rays of sunrise shaft sideways through the surface, dappling him. He shakes his head, face serious, and points upward as he repeats the cutting-throat signal. The surface is dangerous? He makes clawing movements over his chest, and my heart races as an image of Callum flashes into my mind. I shake my head and scull backward. His lips pinch together, jaw tight and frustrated. He jabs a finger at me, then out into the blue.

He doesn't mean . . . I shake my head. No. Not a chance. I can't go out there—I've seen the sharks and jellyfish, and my friend died out there.

No way I am going anywhere with him after last time.

Without warning he dives below and twists behind me, and I spin, panicked. This is it. He's going to block my escape back to shore.

He freezes, hovering, head to one side.

A muffled sound, a voice. It sounds like Iona. She must have followed me into the lagoon. I grind my teeth, eyes clinging to Sea Boy, as if I can hold him there with the force of my gaze, because I don't want him near me, but I do need Iona to see him and know I'm not crazy. If only she'd just shut up . . .

"Aster!" The voice is closer now, accompanied by splashes.

I meet Sea Boy's eyes for less than a second before he spirals backward out of the reef gap, mounts the manta ray, and dissolves into the blue beyond.

20

Sam rides the long route home from the hospital along the towpath, thinking. It's a sunny day and there are lots of dog walkers out, unlike when he met Nygard here. Granda is out of intensive care and stable, but the tumor on his lung has grown. The doctors have said he should be strong enough for chemotherapy in a few weeks' time, but he looked like he'd aged twenty years in a few days, and it terrified Sam. He is on the list for a lung transplant, but it's unlikely. The chemo won't save him—the tumor is inoperable. All it can give is time. Sam can't imagine life without Granda; he's too young, too fit, too full of energy. Granda is the one who met Sam after school when Mom and Dad were working, who always had time for him, who taught him to ride his bike. It is impossible that he won't reach sixty.

Sam has to do something.

Nygard's therapy shrank the tumor. Nygard said if he found Iona he could produce more of this Marisogen without delay. Sam clicks through the gears, standing up on the pedals to go faster. He doesn't know what to do, what to think. He's still shaken from the burglary. What ordinary thief would only steal his old laptop in a shop full of new bikes? There's no evidence to prove the doctor did this, and they found no fingerprints at the shop after the break-in. He swallows, feeling hollow and sick.

He wants Nygard's trial therapy for Granda more than anything.

Maybe stealing his laptop shows Nygard's commitment to finding those girls and Iona because he truly has discovered a cancer treatment that works. Or Nygard didn't steal the laptop at all. Sam could give Nygard Poppy's phone, tell him where he found it, hope it leads him—somehow—to the girls and to making more Marisogen.

Back in his room, Sam opens Mom's laptop, which she's lent

him until the insurance comes through to replace his own. He retrieves the girl's memory card from his desk drawer and slots it into the side of the laptop.

He is struck with an idea. Mom has awesome design software; he's played around with it before. He opens up the program and uses it to flick through the photos of the girls at the camp again, trying to find clues he hasn't noticed, anything that suggests where they planned to go. He lingers on the dimmest one and fiddles with the sensitive controls: brightening, raising the contrast, sharpening. He can see it is the inside of a hut, and there is a laptop with a black screen open on a desk. He trims the photo to show only the laptop and enlarges the image. There's a small yellow rectangle in the corner of the screen. It looks like one of those tiny sticky notes, like he's used in English lessons to mark places in the class book. He zooms in and waits for the photo to adjust and sharpen. There's writing on it—faint, in pencil.

Neatly handwritten numbers.

-164.394531

He scrambles for a pencil, jots them down, then types them in. No results match. What could it be? He checks the photo again to make sure he has the numbers right, then leans back in his chair, scrubs his fingers into his hair, and stares around his bedroom. His eyes catch on the world map on the wall.

He types in the number followed by the word "longitude,"

then "latitude." Nothing. If it is coordinates, then there should be two numbers. But it means *something*—someone wrote it down for a reason.

Sam jogs downstairs to his mom's office, where she has a globe in the corner.

-164. He traces the -165 longitude line with his finger, down from the North Pole. It touches Alaska, then travels through the North Pacific and South Pacific. For the majority of the path of his finger, there's only open ocean. But it isn't *empty* ocean. There are hundreds of small, unnamed islands.

He racks his brain, trying to remember what he learned in geography. *Meridian*. He takes the stairs two at a time and types in "164 meridian" and it comes up with a list of the places the line passes through, the same as he saw on the globe. The number is very specific, to six decimal points. He starts to search again and then stops.

He could go to someone with access to this kind of information, with experience searching for people.

Nygard.

Sam thinks of the girl's phone left on the beach, the footprints. What if Iona found out about Nygard's side project, the Marisogen trial, and stole his work, taking Granda's chances of recovery with her?

Something stopped him from handing over any information

to Nygard last time he saw him, but maybe he was being too suspicious.

Granda might not have much time, and the thought of losing him makes Sam feel hot and frantic. Sam opens his email. If he gives Nygard this information, he can't risk him disappearing forever without treating Granda, so he needs to be smart. When Nygard and Iona were working together they must have chosen that area of forest for their camp because it was so remote. Neither of them wanted what they were doing to be made public. That's the only insurance he's got.

Hi Dr. Nygard,

I have new information I am willing to share with you.
Let me know when you can meet, as soon as possible.

Sam

Sam shifts on the bench, watching the towpath, one hand on the handlebar of his bike, lips moving as he rehearses what he is going to say. He has learned the longitude number by heart, in sets of three. It seemed the safest way.

164.

394.

531.

Should he mention the stolen laptop? He still hasn't decided when Nygard strides up, raising a hand in greeting, then sits down on the bench next to him.

He raises his sunglasses. "Hello, Sam. I was very pleased to hear from you."

Sam turns to look at the doctor. It's warm today, and he's dressed in chino shorts and a gray polo shirt. The breeze ruffles his hair, sun highlighting the silver streaks on either side. He looks ordinary, clean-cut, reliable.

"I have some conditions before I share anything," blurts Sam.

"Whatever you need, Sam," says Nygard. He leans forward, his blue-green eyes on the side of Sam's face.

Sam grips the handlebars of the bike tighter.

"First, that you treat my grandfather at the first opportunity you have. The tumor is coming back, and we don't know how long . . ." Sam is surprised by the clog in his throat.

"I'm very sorry to hear that, Sam. Of course, if the information you give me leads to what I've been looking for, that will be the first thing I will do."

Sam nods.

"Second, that you take me with you," says Sam.

A pause. Nygard's forehead wrinkles in concern. "I'm sure you understand that will depend on—"

"It's not up for discussion. I have to go with you and make sure whatever you find comes back to Granda." Sam swallows.

He forces himself to meet Nygard's calm gaze as he says the part he's been rehearsing.

"If you break these conditions then I will make sure the information I have becomes public knowledge, and I don't think you want that."

Nygard's expression doesn't change as Sam speaks, but then he breaks into a sincere smile. He offers his hand, and after a moment's hesitation, Sam shakes it. Nygard's grip is firm.

"I look forward to working with you, Sam."

21

I sand the wood of the rudder, sawdust tickling my nose. After we'd done the heavy lifting and constructed the frame of the canoe, we made quick progress and are almost finished. It's a basic version of the traditional twin-hulled sailing canoes used by the Polynesians, but it is . . . beautiful. Mostly because it represents me getting to Poppy. We are now waiting on the weather. Today the sun is breaking through the clouds, and the white-topped waves froth gently against the reef rather than spewing plumes of white foam into the air. My eyes catch on the tree trunk with its nine dashes cut into the bark for the nine days we've been here. Iona has named the ring of islands Halo Atoll. This is Halo South, and we need to get to the bigger island, Halo West.

My fear for Poppy continues to shout louder than my fury at Iona. I've buried my feelings about what our aunt did to us very deep so I can cope with her company as we work on the boat every moment the stormy weather allows. It helps that the three of us are so occupied with keeping the camp going and with boatbuilding, we barely get a moment to rest. At the fireside in the evenings Beti works through my curls with coconut oil and a two-pronged comb she carved herself. Chatting about new recipes for kelp and the practicalities of keeping firewood dry stops me from screaming "How could you?" at Iona, over and over.

My stings have now healed well, although there is a patch of swirling scar tissue on one thigh and the opposite shoulder, where the skin is shiny-smooth and a lighter color. The scars make me feel strong. I don't care if they are permanent; it's a good reminder to steer clear of jellyfish. And that I am more difficult to kill than I thought.

Before the rains came I could see nearly across the width of the lagoon, but now there is barely a few meters' visibility. It doesn't stop me from going out there as often as I can, and I'm beginning to associate the water with calm again, rather than danger and grief. Since the morning I saw Sea Boy, when Iona found me swimming at dawn, she sleeps lightly and wakes as soon I do, so I can't get back out there alone and try contacting him again. There was no point in telling either her or Beti that I saw Sea Boy again; they won't believe me.

I sigh and raise my head from my work, smoothing my hand over the wood, hot from sanding. The air is warmer today, and I strip off my poncho. Since the storms, we've been wearing the thin, sandy-colored ponchos that were also in the seemingly bottomless pits of the back pocket of the life vests. The ponchos come down almost to the ground. They are soft on the inside and waterproof on the outside and have hoods with a drawstring for really bad weather. We've needed them.

Iona looks up from where she is sanding the other end of the boat.

"Weather has brightened up," she says. "I'll take a look."

I nod. Iona lays her tools in the hollow inside the hull. I don't follow, but I do watch her leave. I know she'll walk to the rocks at the far end of the beach, like she does every day. She has a sort of straight-backed gliding walk. Mom could walk around the house doing chores with a book balanced on her head. She'd have Poppy and me in fits of laughter. I hate it when Iona and Mom merge in my mind, but I can't always stop it.

You think far too much.

At least it's Poppy's voice this time, not Mom's. If something happens to Poppy, I'll never have spoken to her about Mom—we will never have remembered her together.

I can't think like that. Not about Poppy, not even for a minute. I rub the bark roughly, concentrating on the ache in my shoulder, the smell of the hot wood, the grating sound. *Please let today be the day we get to you, Poppy. We've got barely anything to pack and nothing to stop us. I'm coming for you, Popstar.*

We leave the following day. The island retreats into the distance, and my hair whips back from my face. I shake the sail as Iona taught me, thrilled by the speed when the wind catches. Iona makes a hand signal from where she sits at the back of the central platform, working the tiller, steering. I allow the rope to slide past my gloved hands a little, slowing us down. We are wearing the gray bodysuits we arrived in to protect against sunburn and the gloves to guard against the ropes. The life jackets have been stripped of tubes and the pockets emptied, and we wear those too to act as flotation aids if we fall in. Our knives and machetes are strapped to our belts. Beti and Iona wove baseball-style caps from dried grasses, which we've jammed on our heads to shield against the glare from the morning sun on the sea, strings tied under our chins to stop them blowing off.

We must look utterly weird.

Beti tries to tip her cap up, and when she nearly loses it in the wind, I release a burst of laughter. It is a strange feeling. None of us has laughed much since we arrived. But now our canoe is sailing, and we are on our way to find the others.

The sails were by far the trickiest part of the boat. Iona told us she packed thin, high-tech sails into the equipment trunk that was dropped on the other island. We've had to improvise with a traditional method, making them from woven grasses treated with resin. They rattle and the wind whistles through the gaps in the weave, but we are making excellent time, tracking along the same sandbank I followed to the mangrove island. The waves break along its line, so Iona holds a course slightly inside it, toward the deeper, dark water in the center of the atoll.

We pass the mangrove island, giving it a wide berth.

"I can't believe you swam this far on your own," says Beti.

She takes the rope from me just as my arms begin to ache. I stare at the mangrove roots tangling over the rocks and the few palms spiking from the center.

"I can't believe it either," I say, spotting the place where Sea Boy and I balanced on the mangrove roots.

The sail makes a creaking sound, and I grab the rope above Beti's wrist to loosen the tension.

Halo West is now racing toward us, and the trees along this side of the coast rise up from a rocky shore. Like our island, this one has a lagoon facing the center of the atoll. I put my hands over the peak of the cap and stare until my eyes water. My heart is almost in my throat and thumping hard.

There is a possibility they aren't there; Halo West is only the most likely option. But what if none of us ended up where we were supposed to be? I roll my tense shoulders and dismiss the thought.

I join Iona at the tiller. From here the other islands of the atoll are visible, hazy mounds on the horizon. It's good to see the opposite side of the island ring; it makes me feel less isolated.

"How deep is the center?" I say.

"The water is dark, so it's hard to say," says Iona.

I nod, thinking of Sea Boy. I could talk about him now; it doesn't matter how crazy Iona and Beti think I am now that the boat is built and I'm here, about to find my sister.

I *could* talk about Sea Boy. But I don't.

We reach the end of the rocky shore that faces our island. On the other side is the bay, the Halo West lagoon. Beti takes the sail again, and I sit at the front, spray soaking me, desperate to catch the first glimpse of their camp. Disappointment bursts in my chest as we round the spur of rocks and the curve of the bay spreads out in front of us, pristine and deserted.

"Can you see anything?" says Beti, her words whipped from her mouth by the wind.

I shake my head.

She lets out the sail, and the boat slows.

"They may have set up camp farther inland," says Iona. Her voice is flat and her face expressionless. I don't like this.

This lagoon is teardrop-shaped, sheltered by a hook of sturdier reef on the round side with a flat sandbar enclosing the other end, getting shallower at the point. We beach the boat on the wide sandbar and tug it over into tranquil lagoon waters only a meter or so deep. It's a natural harbor. We remove our hats, grab our snorkeling gear, and fan out; it's quicker to swim than wade through the warm shallows. I'm the fastest swimmer, but the others keep up because I stop frequently to slide up my goggles and scan the empty beach.

The sand looks smooth. No sign of anyone having been here.

I don't want to consider what this means.

Iona wades out of the water without turning, and fear rises to the surface of my skin like a toxic sweat.

Beti follows her, panting, and points back at the lagoon. "You said they've got supplies here to start the oyster farms, the mariculture," she says. "Wouldn't we see the ropes across the lagoon?"

Iona doesn't reply, marching ahead.

My breaths are too shallow and too quick and my legs are trembling as if they've taken on a life of their own and don't want me to go any farther. I count in my head, force air through my nose on the inhale. *Three in, six out*. I can't panic now. I have to be strong for Poppy.

Callum died.

What if they all died?

Don't think about it.

We reach the center of the bay, and the three of us are silent. The sand is scattered with signs of life: seaweed, and tiny shells.

Not a footprint in sight.

22

Iona jogs up the last of the beach, crunching her footprints deep into that horribly unblemished sand. If they aren't here, they are on another island. They must be. But I can't persuade myself it is true. Horrors race through my mind too fast, like an old-fashioned movie reel. They all got sick and died. They drowned on the way to shore, floating in the sea in Iona's stupid prototype life vests. Torn apart by predators. Whatever happened to

Callum could have happened to them. I mouth the words: "Please. Please. Please." *Not Poppy.*

Numbness creeps through me, and although it holds my panic back, I know it will only be temporary.

I follow Iona into the trees. There is no natural clearing like there is on our island. It is shady as she leads us deeper, drawing her machete and hacking at the thick creepers and ferns. We've only ventured this far inland on Halo South to find the wood for timber. How can the others be in this tangled undergrowth?

"Where are they?" I say.

Iona doesn't turn and ignores me when I repeat the question. A dark patch of sweat soaks the back of her T-shirt between her shoulder blades. Beti draws her machete and helps Iona slice at the undergrowth. As I reach out to take Iona's shoulder and demand that she tell me what she's looking for, she stops. A low noise rumbles in her throat as she starts uncovering something. She rips off vines and creepers to reveal a silver box about the size of one of those top-opening chest freezers, the surfaces dulled with green. It must be the equipment chest, but the fact it's covered in undergrowth is further evidence that they aren't here, and my heart sinks further. Iona left this here some time ago, when she planted the fruit trees on the islands.

Iona opens a large flip-up catch and slides out a pole. The

chest springs open a little, and she lifts it the rest of the way and then turns, sweat running down her cheek.

"They haven't been here," she says. She pinches her top lip and blinks rapidly.

"Where is my sister?" I say, voice rising. "Another beach?"

"No. They would have found the equipment chest if they were on this island. No. I think they are still . . . safe," she says. I feel like she's calculating something.

"Safe?" says Beti. "How can you know that?"

As Beti's voice cracks, fear floods me. Beti's confidence in Iona despite everything has kept me going.

"There's things you need to know," says Iona.

She leans over the silver chest and rakes around deep inside. I peer over her shoulder and see ropes, fabric, tools, and plastic boxes of different sizes. She brings out what looks like a black plastic backpack and a diving mask with thick rubber tubes snaking out of it. She hands the bundle to me, and I almost drop it. It's heavier than it looks. She passes Beti two pairs of black flippers.

"Please, Iona. I do not get this. Shouldn't we try the next island?" says Beti.

Iona takes out a second bundle of diving equipment and closes the lid.

"Back to the beach. I'll explain," she says, and before we can argue she's striding back along the path she cut. The trees open out, and I spot the boat bobbing at the edge of the reef where we left it.

Iona drops the diving equipment on the sand, and I do the same. Beti takes my hand and holds it tight. We both believed the others would be on this island—we made ourselves believe it.

"Everything I told you about the reasons we came here is true," says Iona. She pauses, meets my eyes, and licks her lips. "The others are safe. In the container. The one that you saw on the back of *Deep Retreat*."

I feel my face crumple in disbelief. Of all the things I was expecting her to say, that wasn't one of them.

"What do you mean?" I recall the huge, beige metal box looming on the back of the boat. My sister is in that container? It's been ten days. Iona's not making any sense; she's finally lost it.

"There's something I haven't told you about the specifics of the therapy at Wildhaven. I studied certain animals that show a resistance to cancer. My theory was that this was linked to their ability to hibernate. In short, we found a way to integrate their DNA with yours."

I force my breaths through my nose to slow them down.

"This will take a while to sink in. The genetic therapy deactivates the cancer gene when *combined* with hibernation. Your heartbeat was slowed to less than a couple of beats a minute, and your lungs were filled with an oxygenated liquid so you didn't need to breathe."

I shake my head, not able to process this new insanity. This can't be true. Then I remember Beti when Callum and I found her, how she had seemed dead, not breathing, her heartbeat so impossibly slow. I was certain she'd spent too long without oxygen.

Beti speaks in a slow quiet voice. "Was this why we wore the wristbands at night, in Wildhaven?"

"Yes. I'd been monitoring your sleep patterns since the gene insertion, and you all experienced periods of decelerated heart rate, breathing, and body temperature during rest. All I had to do was induce a deep sleep."

"But when we signed up for the therapy you never said anything about hibernation," says Beti.

"Beti, it is perfectly safe. You know I would never consider anything that wasn't."

An image of Callum, broken on the beach, flashes into my mind. *Perfectly safe.* The same words she said to us on the boat the last time I was with Poppy.

"Where's this container now? Where's Poppy *now*?" My hands shake, and I ball them into fists.

Iona points out to sea. "Out there. Submerged about six meters down."

I remember the blue gunk we coughed up when we washed up on the beach that first day. My eyelids taped closed. The tubes in our arms. I'm going to have to believe her, although my rational mind doesn't want to.

"Then why aren't we with them?" I say.

Iona's hesitation activates my thumping heart.

"The pods should have released at the same time, but in the case of a malfunction, they were programmed to discharge early." She takes a deep breath. "It is more likely they are still in hibernation than on one of the further islands."

Malfunction. The word reverberates in my head.

"Why didn't you just tell us this before? Why did you make us believe they were on this island?" I say.

"I thought it most likely that they were. And either way, we needed to concentrate on building the canoe."

Iona says this firmly, and it's clear she's not sorry. She's always managed the information, told us only what she felt we needed to know. I can't understand how she has such an unshakeable belief that what she is doing is right.

She lifts one set of the diving gear she brought from the chest.

"Aster, you dive with me to the container, as you're the strongest swimmer. Beti will look after the canoe at the surface."

"Fine," says Beti, her voice stronger now. She grips my hand tight, then releases it so I can lift the scuba mask and backpack thing. I feel a clank and guess an oxygen tank must be inside. This is all happening too quickly—I still feel like Poppy must be here on the island. I try to meet Beti's eyes, but she is staring intently at the side of Iona's face. She has always believed in Iona through everything, and I can't tell how much these new revelations have shaken her faith.

"I'll go over the basics with you now in the lagoon, Aster, and if the weather holds, we'll dive to the container first thing in the morning," says Iona.

I shake my head but follow her down to the lagoon.

I don't enjoy my crash course in scuba diving; the gear is bulky, and the mouthpiece—regulator—grinds against my gums. Iona explains that the tanks are called rebreathers and are military spec. In other circumstances I'd be interested to learn how they recycle our exhaled breath. But I'm more focused on how the gas mixture makes me light-headed, how when I breathe too quickly the equipment judders. I'm exhausted by the time Iona is satisfied that I'm capable.

Later we sit on the sand by the campfire, eating fish skewered on sharp sticks. I prod at the fire for something to do, and it crackles and spews sparks. We've set up a low sleeping tent on the sand using tarpaulins from the equipment chest. I find myself thinking fondly of Halo South, where our camp had been homey in comparison and we'd let ourselves settle into the belief that the others were just a boat hop away.

Iona stands and stretches.

I can't believe she did this to us. I remember Beti's slack face as I tried to breathe into her, her lungs blocked with gunk. That's probably what Poppy looks like now, and the grip of panic tightens around my throat at the thought. Iona thinks that injecting us with animal genes and putting us into hibernation is *acceptable*. She put us into a state of living death, in a box, underwater.

I remember Mom once told me her sister never got over their parents' deaths.

And I thought *I* was struggling with the grief process.

"So does Dr. Nygard know about this . . . hibernation?" I say.

"In the early stages of our research, we noticed changes in metabolism and sleep patterns in candidates after the therapy injection, but the cancer genes remained unchanged. I suggested that there were two parts to the process, that it was the hibernation itself that deactivated the cancer genes. He wouldn't consider it, and we never discussed it again. Looking back, I think this must have been when he began his own research, started collecting the extra blood samples. I sourced the components for the hibernation pods inside the container over the course of the last three years without his knowledge."

"So *now* we are free of cancer because we've been through this hibernation?"

Iona nods.

"And you think Dr. Nygard is still looking for us?" says Beti.

"It's like I told you. There was no point in collecting blood samples until after the hibernation period, as the results wouldn't show up until then. He was doing something else with your blood."

"Could he have been using it to move on to the next stage you talked about, to make a cure for people who already had cancer? People would pay any price, they wouldn't care where it came from, from animals or blood or whatever," I say. "This Nygard would be rich."

"Are you saying we have a priceless cancer cure in our *blood*?" says Beti.

Iona sighs, gathers together her pile of fish bones, and throws them in the fire.

"I'm not saying that, Beti. I hope the research has implications for existing cancer sufferers in the future, but that's not something I've investigated yet."

Iona's face is serene, and I can't understand it. Tomorrow we'll dive to this container where my eleven-year-old sister is barely alive. My anger rises, and I don't fight it this time.

"How are you any different from him?" I say, the words flowing hot and fast. "You might have gotten consent for an injection—from the others at least—but not for this hibernation thing. You took our choice and then literally took us—away."

Iona stands, gathering the sheet we each packed around her shoulders. Her voice is calm, firm.

"I have *given* you everything. You would have died of cancer, Aster. I don't know what type of cancer it would have been; I don't know when it would have taken you, whether you'd have been young or old. But you had the genetic marker, and now you don't. I saw orphaned teenagers that I could help, plus the chance of developing a future treatment that could change the face of medicine. Nygard was *using* you."

My voice is quieter now. "You tricked us."

"Would you have agreed to it if I had told you everything?"

I glare at her but can't answer. I don't know, and the question isn't fair. It also isn't the point.

Iona sighs. "One day you will understand. And I want you to know, before I considered any of this, I did test it. On myself."

Beti and I stare at her. That doesn't make me feel any better.

Iona continues to stand, sucking in the side of her cheek. I don't want to talk about this anymore; I just want to get to Poppy. All I've wanted from the moment I woke up in this place is to get to Poppy.

"So we'll dive down to the container once the sun is up?" I say.

"Yes." Iona meets my eyes, then Beti's, then looks inland to the jungle. "And I want you to know that in the bottom of the equipment chest there is a small black box. Inside I've left a memory stick. It holds all the research Nygard and I did together: my own notes, and the results of your monitoring. It's all there."

23

Beti operates the tiller, and I take the sail. We progress as slowly as possible without the boat becoming unstable, scanning below for the darker water that signals the underwater cliff dropping away into the central pit of the atoll. Iona explains that the container is only around ten meters in from the cliff, about six meters deep. She describes how she used a specialized cargo winch on the boat to lower it into the water over a grove of tall brown kelp that would help camouflage it.

"So you joined us in the container once it was down there?" says Beti.

Iona sits on the hull, surveying the water. She turns to meet Beti's eyes and then mine. "I'd already had the hibernation treatment once, so I considered waiting on the island, overseeing your release from the container when the time came. But if Jonathan found me, he'd know you were nearby. I decided my place was with you."

She holds up her wrists. The tiny scars the tubes made mirror mine and Beti's. I'd never noticed them before.

Suddenly the water turns from deep turquoise to navy blue. "Here," I call out. "That must be the cliff."

Beti lets the sail flap free. "Shall I drop anchor?" she says.

Iona is already putting on her snorkel gear. "No—keep the sail slack and use the oars to steady us. Might not be exactly the right place, but we're near. We'll snorkel until we find it, and then you'll need to cast anchor so we can dive."

I take a deep breath in and blow it back out, settling my shoulders. I zip up my silver suit and put on my snorkel gear. The boat rocks as Iona steps into the water and I follow. We float across the surface as we survey the bottom.

The seabed here is lifeless compared to nearer the islands, like the surface of the moon, with only a few red starfish to break up the monotony. The cliff edge drops away to the center of the atoll, and the fathomless blue sends sparks of fear up my spine.

We swim on, kicking our legs hard, keeping our arms by our sides so we have an uninterrupted view. Iona points out a forest of waving brown fronds in front of us, and we both surface. She signals to Beti on the boat, water dripping from her short twists of hair, face set and determined. Before I can say anything she dives down into the kelp grove, parting the rubbery stalks with her hands. Her flippers disappear into the waving forest, and I don't follow but bob at the surface, clear of the seaweed. I feel a prickle at my neck, a sensation of being watched. With a deep breath through the snorkel I dive and spin around. The darkness of the center of the atoll is on my left, the lighter blue of the shallower water on my right. I stare into the darkness, sure I saw a shifting shape in the murk. Nothing. Is it Sea Boy?

Just as I'm beginning to worry that Iona has been gone too long, she sweeps upward out of the kelp and breaks the surface. She catches her breath and nods. The container is down there.

Iona hovers above the container, looking like a gray-and-black insect with the looping tubes and visor of the scuba suit. The beige metal box blends in with the seafloor, and the kelp fronds form a canopy above, making it invisible from the surface and from the air. I join Iona, blowing through my nose and pinching it at the same time until my ears pop and the pressure in my head eases. I'm not enjoying my first open-water scuba dive. It is nothing like swimming freely; the mouthpiece makes me want to gag, and the backpack limits my movement as it cleanses the gas I breathe out so I can breathe the same air over and over. I have barely any peripheral vision in the scuba mask. A shoal of shimmering fish darts out of the kelp grove, giving me a jolt. Anything could hide in these dense fronds. Iona grabs the specialized whiteboard and pen that are clipped to the front of her backpack and writes:

Ready?

My mind leaps back to Mom in her hospital bed, writing on her pad, and I push the memory aside and give Iona the OK sign with my hand, even though nothing about this is OK. I don't know how to prepare for seeing Poppy, unconscious, hibernating.

We are deeper than I've ever been, and although we catch glimpses of the flickering surface above through the swaying kelp, things are different down here. The water is colder, the colors faded so Iona's skin is a sickly gray. Deathly.

My pulse is in my throat, rushing in my ears. I breathe too quickly, and the air supply judders.

Iona lays her hand flat against the container, resting it there, touching. She nods and beckons me, indicating I should do the same. I place the palm of my hand on the metal, and it feels cold through my gloves. It vibrates very slightly, and I think I understand. Whatever powers this thing and keeps Poppy and the others' life support going is turned on. I don't want to think about what would have happened if the power had failed.

Iona scoops away puffs of silt from the ridged metal, then lifts a recessed handle and pulls. The hatch opens easily with a bigger cloud of silt but needs to be held open; it's on some sort of spring that closes it automatically. My eyes cling to the slice of darkness inside the container, blacker than ink. Iona lights her flashlight and indicates for me to hold the handle. We planned this on the surface—she'll go in first, I'll slide through after. When the door closes, we need to be prepared for the dark. That's why we already have our flashlights lit.

Iona points at her board again, the same word.

Ready?

A shadow passes over the sun sparkling above. I stare from side to side, looking for the source, forcing my breath to slow down.

But there's nothing to see now—it was just the rippling kelp. When I nod to Iona, she slips inside feetfirst. The dark swallows her legs and torso, then her head, and before I can think too much I slide in after her. I'm not usually scared of the dark, but this is completely disorienting, and when Iona reaches for me, I cling tightly to her arm before catching hold of my flashlight and angling it around. My skin puckers in the cold, and a hum passes through the water, a low, almost imperceptible vibration.

At first it is hard to make sense of what I'm seeing, but then I make out what Iona called the hibernation pods. They are rectangular with rounded edges, a couple of meters long and less than a meter wide. Their dull metal catches the flashlight beam as I scan the underwater room. The pods line the walls, like ancient Egyptian mummy cases in a museum. I swim closer. Tubes snake from the tops of the pods into the wall above them. My turbulence disturbs the water, and the door of the nearest pod swings open a fraction. I breathe sharply, and Iona is in front of me. She opens the door and shines in her flashlight. Empty. Wires and tubes nestle at the top end, curled over each other like a sleeping octopus. My mind spins back to the first day on the island, waking on the beach, the tubes plugged into our wrists, coiling up our arms and into the top of the life vests. I remember the empty sockets in the back of the canvas at the neck.

My skin tingles; waves crash inside my ears.

The door of the pod is on the same sort of spring as the hatch and closes when she releases it.

She points to herself and to me. Yes. We knew there were four empty ones, ours plus Callum's and Beti's. She quickly pulls open the next three. And then we both see it, the beams of our flashlights crisscrossing. The next pod is also ajar.

Iona and I hold each other tight, forearm-to-forearm, in the dark. All I can hear is the container's hum and my own hissing breaths through the regulator in my mouth.

It doesn't matter that the power is on, that the hatch is undisturbed; the technology malfunctioned anyway.

The hibernation pods have become coffins.

This whole box is a group tomb.

I detach myself from Iona because I have to know. If this experiment failed and they are all dead, I need to see for myself, no matter how bad it is. My flashlight flicks erratically around the container as I kick across to the gaping pod and haul it open.

Empty.

No Poppy.

I fling open the next and the next. Empty, all of them empty, but I can't stop until I have opened every single one. Then I scan across the ceiling, the floor. Iona swims to the wall on my right, next to the last pod, and starts feeling along the wall. She locates a notch and opens a small door to reveal a control panel, each button and lever dimly lit. It looks basic, military. Three large levers in a row at the top: one red, one blue, one black. Below them are rows of metal flip switches like you might expect to see in the cockpit of a plane. I hover closer. On a small digital screen at the top is the number 276. Iona shakes her head. I don't know what it means of course, because I've never known what any of this means.

All I know is Poppy isn't dead.

Because Poppy isn't here.

24

Sam's eyes flicker open, and it takes a moment to remember that he's aboard Nygard's yacht. The doctor calculated that the only place along that precise line of longitude that was plausible was a tiny uninhabited atoll in an isolated stretch of the South Pacific. They should reach the coordinates today.

Sam didn't like lying to his parents about where he was going. Mom and Dad think he's with a couple of mates for spring break, riding the mountain trails, camping in the bush.

He's done that kind of thing before and warned them he probably wouldn't have a signal or charge on his phone, but he's only got a week left before they start to worry. He hopes he'll be back by then.

He peers out of the small window in his cabin. The sea is calm, the sky the deep blue before dawn. The muffled voices of Nygard and his cronies come through the thin ceiling. He's grown to intensely dislike the two men Nygard has hired. They are cousins, around Nygard's age with matching gelled-back dark hair. One is tanned and wrinkled as a walnut and the other has teeth that are far too white. Nygard did tell him their names, but Sam thinks of them as Tan and Teeth. They think of nothing but hunting. Birds, fish, turtles—no living thing is safe, and they have a freaky array of harpoons and knives. When the yacht slows, they pull on black wet suits and snorkel gear and go diving. The first day they caught a huge sailfish with a beautiful rainbow fin and left it thrashing on deck for ten minutes before Nygard finally whacked the poor thing over the head.

Teeth and Tan don't think much of Sam either; they can't get a grasp on his lack of enthusiasm for death. He's tried to stay out of their way, and the yacht is big enough that it's just about possible. Nygard himself is polite to Sam, and whenever they talk his eyebrows still tilt up in the middle in that trustworthy way. But he hasn't given a straight answer to a single one of Sam's questions about what the plan is if they actually find Iona. He's determined to retrieve his research, but how?

There's a knot in Sam's stomach, and it has been steadily tightening.

He sometimes hears his granda's voice. *You can tell a lot about a bloke from who he hangs out with. Steer well clear, kiddo.*

Why did Nygard bring him at all? Sam made that half-hearted attempt to threaten exposing his work if he didn't take him. He also left a note in his desk drawer with the coordinates of the island and Nygard's name so that if he didn't come back, his parents would be sure to search his room and find it. At the time, this had seemed smart, but now—not so much. When Nygard gets what he came for he could throw Sam overboard and disappear, change his name, never return to New Zealand.

Sam sometimes catches Nygard looking at him and has the unsettling impression that he hasn't decided what to do with him. Yet.

Sam pulls on a T-shirt and stumbles up the stairs and out onto the deck. The approaching sunrise is a bleached-out patch of blue on the horizon. For the last few days it's begun to feel like there is nothing but this. Half the world is sea, the other half is sky, and Nygard's yacht is a speck riding the line in between. Sam scratches his chin. He forgot his razor in the rush to leave and has a surprising amount of blond stubble. All his 30 SPF sunscreen is finished, and his hair feels like straw from the hours spent on deck. In the cabin's bathroom mirror he barely looks like himself.

By midafternoon, Sam is shirtless in the roiling heat, a floppy fisherman's hat on his head. His eyes water from staring into the binoculars.

He follows the dark line of the horizon for the thousandth time. No sign of land.

He drops the binoculars so they rest on his chest and flops down on one of the padded benches on the rear deck. The yacht is set up for luxury cruises—probably involving harpoon hunting—with faux-leather seats, polished wooden decking, everything else either gleaming white or chrome. He rolls flat on his back, pulling down the brim of his hat, resting his eyes. Every muscle aches. Bright blobs travel across the backs of his eyelids.

Teeth calls out, "We have visuals."

Sam springs up and rams the binoculars into the bridge of his nose. An unevenness at the horizon. A break in the flat sea. The atoll.

They pass through the channel between the nearest two islands, and Nygard directs all of them to search for signs of life on the beaches with their binoculars. There's nothing on the first two islands. They pass closer to each one and scan the sand for footprints, the tree line for hammocks, or signs of man-made construction of any kind. They seem untouched. Nygard wears a loose blue shirt and khaki shorts. His dark baseball cap is pulled low, and his eyes glint beneath the brim.

It is Tan's turn to call out. "Unidentified object at twelve o'clock."

Sam rolls his eyes. These guys speak like military wannabes, but it's pretty obvious neither has ever been in the armed forces. Sam walks along the side of the cabin to the front of the boat, scanning the horizon. He spots a tiny dark speck, aims his binoculars, and fiddles with the focus dial. A boat? Way out here, in the middle of this uninhabited atoll, is a sailing boat.

The engine revs, and as they close in on the boat, it becomes clear how tiny it actually is: a wooden canoe with two hulls and one sail in between and a single person on deck.

Sam can't hear what Nygard and the others are saying over the roaring engine. He watches the boat with a sick feeling in his stomach, more than simple anticipation. He brought Nygard and these two trigger-happy jokers out here with no clue of what they've actually got planned.

Nygard joins him as the yacht draws closer to the sailing boat, which isn't attempting to move, the sail flapping pointlessly in the wind. It looks like the person on deck is a black girl or woman wearing a gray wetsuit and a straw hat. She's facing away. Nygard's binoculars are high spec, very powerful, and

Sam guesses she doesn't even know they are there, unless she has similar equipment.

As Sam watches, two more figures flop aboard the sailing boat. It looks like they're rigged in black scuba gear. Where did *they* come from?

Nygard calls out. "Slow down. Turn on the sonar and scan the area. And get kitted up."

PART FOUR
DROWNING

25

Back on board the sailing canoe, I strip off the scuba mask and mouthpiece and crumple under the weight of the rebreather backpack without the water to support it on my back. For a few seconds I lie there, cheek against the warm wood of the deck, listening to Iona tell Beti that the others weren't in the container. Then I sit up and unfasten the buckles at my waist and chest, shrugging free from the kit. I take a grateful gulp of the water Beti offers me, even though I feel sick with anxiety.

Poppy wasn't at the island, and she isn't in the container. Iona doesn't *know* where my sister is, and I can't bear to hear her admit it.

"Then where are they?" says Beti. Her voice is abrupt, and she folds her arms. I sense her last threads of faith in Iona dissolving, and it shakes me.

Iona swigs water and swipes a hand over her face. "The guidance systems in the life jackets are programmed to find land—"

I interrupt as a thought enters my head: "The number on that control panel thing—276—what does that mean?"

Iona doesn't get a chance to reply. The boat lurches, and we all crouch to keep our balance. Beti crawls to the edge and peers over.

"Did you see that? Something in the water—there."

I spin around. A dark shadow beneath the surface. More than one. Seven, eight, no—nine shapes, gliding together in a group, almost a formation.

Beti skips to the platform at the back. "Might be a pod of dolphins. No, look—they're diamond-shaped."

I spot the rippling white undersurfaces of their huge wings. Manta rays. Is it Sea Boy? If so, then he's not alone.

"Wait. It's—"

Iona voice interrupts me, calm. "The two of you haul up the anchor, then be ready at the tiller." She is already shaking the sail so the woven reeds crackle. "They're pretty big; we don't want to be capsized."

The manta rays sweep back and forth alongside us. Beti and I haul the rock we've been using as an anchor up on deck, and the boat surges forward.

A squatting figure bursts out of the water.

Sea Boy. He flicks black hair from his eyes and crouches low on the back of the manta ray, using one hand to balance, his feet covered by the lapping waves. Others surface behind him. Eight more, crouching on the backs of the manta rays as they skim the surface. All have the same dark slices of gills at the tops of their chests. They wear rags and are armed with knives, black spears, and slim white harpoons.

I'm aware of Iona and Beti's voices but can't make out what they are saying.

Sea Boy tilts his head as he looks at me and waves his arm at the others behind him, gesturing for them to lower their weapons.

At Sea Boy's shoulder there is a brown-skinned girl with ragged red dreadlocks interwoven with shells. Puckered scars dot her stomach. When she raises a handful of sea urchin spines, my hand darts to my knife. I lock eyes with her—and I know I've locked eyes with this girl before. In the cabin of the *Deep Retreat*, with the gas swirling around us. How can this be the same girl?

Beti calls out, "Sunee? Talal?"

Beti *knows* them. From Wildhaven, but they can't be. These

aren't the students I last saw in the boat cabin, dressed in the gray suits, excited about a snorkeling trip—these are sea people, riding on manta rays.

The boy next to Sea Boy holds a length of wood with a shard of glass embedded in the end, glinting in the sun. Are they attacking us? My mind is working too slowly. I see more familiar faces but no names spring to mind. I raise both of my hands, palms out.

Threat fizzles like electricity in the air.

My eyes switch back to Sea Boy.

Iona scrambles across to grasp the rope, and the boat catches the wind and lurches toward Sea Boy and the others. She calls out more names and at the same time, the rock we're using as an anchor rolls across the deck and hits my foot hard. I yelp and stagger back, but the rope is tangled around my ankle. I try to catch my balance, but I'm right at the edge of the deck, arms wheeling. I tumble backward into the water and surface, spluttering. Beti crouches above on deck, only a meter away, and she stretches out her hand to me, calling my name in panic. I kick hard and strain my fingers toward hers. Then something constricts around my lower leg and I am yanked down without a chance to gasp a breath.

I reach out for the surface as the anchor drags me down, spinning deeper and deeper.

26

I kick and kick, trying to free myself from the rope, but it only winds tighter around my ankle. I can't see through the clouds of bubbles. Are we still above the drop-off, or has the boat drifted to the deeper water in the center of the atoll?

The rock answers me by landing with a thud on the seabed. I jerk up like I'm on a reverse bungee and then hang there, tethered by the rope at my ankle. I see dark, waving brown. I'm at the edge of the kelp forest, and I look up through the fronds.

The rays of sunlight are cut through by the silhouette of the rope binding me to the boat. I'll have run out of air by the time Iona gets her dive gear back on.

Every fiber of my body wants to struggle and thrash my way free, but I force myself to fall still. My chest is constricted; all my air has already gone in the panic.

My knife.

I grab it, sunlight glinting off the blade.

I will cut myself free. I can do this.

Reach. Kick. Breathe.

Yes, Mom. I know.

I jackknife down, fronds of kelp brushing my face. The yellow nylon rope is thin but very strong, and it is wrapped twice around my ankle. I aim for the section of rope below where it is drawn taut, swinging from side to side. My blade slips up and down a few times before I manage to make a notch and start sawing, strands of rope springing free. My lungs burn; I saw faster and another thread of the rope pings free. I'm over halfway through, got to keep going. But black spots creep across my vision, and my hand trembles. Panic surges through my body.

I'm not alone. Sea Boy appears through the kelp fronds. I meet his eyes, beseeching.

Help me.

He shakes his head once, shoots forward and grabs my wrist, stopping my hand.

Stopping me cutting myself free.

I writhe in his grip and remember when we were below the jellyfish. Once he got hold of me—he was so strong. I twist, my spare hand finds purchase on a thick kelp root, and I kick out my free leg, my heel connecting hard with his stomach. Sea Boy releases my wrist and spins into the kelp, doubled over in pain. I've dropped my knife, and it's out of reach.

I'm going to breathe in water; this is it, finally it.

Reach.

I reach across to my other hip and draw my machete. I'm not finished yet—

Someone yanks the weapon from my grip.

The sea people hover all around me now. Not sea people—the kids from Wildhaven. But that can't be true because why would they watch me drown like this? Sea Boy reaches out a hand as if to reassure me, and I don't get this—he stopped my escape. I shake my head and wheel backward, and then my body convulses, ankle jerking at the rope. I have to get free.

Reach. Kick. Breathe.

I'm underwater, Mom!

Breathe.

The kelp parts, and the sun shoots a halo of shards.

Mom, I can't. I give a silent wail, and the extent of my grief engulfs me. *I lost Poppy, and I can't do any of this without you. Mom—come back, please! I need you now . . .*

Her voice again. *Breathe.*

I have no choice. I suck in the sea in a long murderous gulp. The water invades my nose, my throat, my chest, and every muscle tenses in anticipation of the pain, of the end.

Nothing. Silence.

The sea is salty and cool, heavy and so very wrong inside me.

I've drowned. Finally, after everything, I've drowned.

So why doesn't it hurt?

I open my eyes. Sea Boy's hands are wrapped around both my clenched fists. He meets my gaze and then nods to my chest.

I look down.

Adrenaline hits, and I claw at the fabric of my swimsuit, pulling it lower.

My skin.

Indentations have appeared, slim channels between my ribs growing deeper and pinker. It is as if an invisible knife is slicing the skin open from the center of my chest to the outside of my ribs. There is no blood. It hurts, but in a new way, like scratching an itch a little too hard. Panic thuds through my veins, flashes across my skin. I cycle my free leg and flail out. Instinct overrides every other thought. I need air, light, the surface. What I'm seeing isn't real.

The black spots join and spread until everything is dark.

My eyes spring open to find my chin tilted back, firm fingers at my jaw, and a face very close to mine, his lips hovering over my mouth. I instinctively push hard against Sea Boy's chest. My rib cage drops, and water passes out of the slits in my chest. I touch my—*gills?*—feeling the warm puffs of exhaled water.

And my chest rises, bringing in a fresh inhalation of sea . . . I am breathing. Underwater.

Sea Boy's eyebrows arch high, his face a mask of concern.

Time is suspended.

He *knew*. Beneath the jellyfish he knew this was possible. He wasn't trying to drown me.

He knew I *couldn't* drown.

I hold out my shaking hand to him. He grips my forearm and I grip his. I steady myself and stare around me at the others. Poppy, where is Poppy? Oxygen from the water hits my brain, new connections firing.

The girl with the red hair collects my machete and knife from the seabed and hands them to me. I slot them back into my belt with trembling fingers.

Sunee. I nod my thanks to her.

I scan each of the underwater people, searching for Poppy's face as I try to work out what this all means. They look so different: muscled, ragged, and fierce.

I recognize some of them.

Boy.

Iona knows them. Before I fell, I heard her call out to them.

Another boy—Darnell?

White girl.

The Wildhaven kids weren't in the pods. They have gills.

Girl with brown skin, not Poppy.

Boy.

I have gills.

Boy—Dimi.

Girl with black skin.

That's all of them. Eight plus Sea Boy.

It's a group of Wildhaven kids, about half of them. And Poppy's not with them. Where are the others?

Without thinking about it, my chest is gently sucking water in and easing it out.

I focus on Sea Boy, still gripping my arm. One of the kids swims down and slices through the rope holding me to the anchor. I rise up out of the kelp.

I'm free, I'm flying, I'm impossible.

Sea Boy is wearing the remnants of one of the gray suits we arrived in, the suit I am wearing now, but only the ragged torso of it, arms cut off. I reach out with one finger and touch the zip, low between his ribs. I feel the warmth of the water leaving his gills and snatch my hand back.

I remember the glove I found on the mangrove island: worn, old, disintegrating. It must have belonged to one of the Wildhaven kids.

How long have they been here?

A lot longer than ten days.

A clicking sound disrupts my thoughts. It's the same sound Sea Boy made when he called the manta ray. The girl with the red hair works her jaw, and a manta ray speeds toward her. Now the others are also clicking—whirling onto their mantas, sweeping away.

Above, a figure descends through the kelp toward me, the tube curling from her mouth. Iona in her scuba gear.

Sea Boy tries to shake free of me, but I grip his arm tighter. He points to the surface and to his ear. I can't hear anything, and I refuse to let him go. He must know where Poppy is, and I plead with my eyes, mouth her name. His face crumples, but he shakes his head as he peels my hand off his wrist. Iona drifts clumsily down toward me.

Sea Boy's manta ray sweeps up to him and he mounts. I struggle to keep upright in the turbulence from the huge fish, then strike out toward him. The others are disappearing toward the center of the atoll, and he follows.

I race after him, even though I know it's hopeless. I try to build some speed with my butterfly kick, but the seawater flowing through my open mouth is disorienting. I'll never catch Sea Boy, and then I will never find Poppy.

I stop to stare as he banks around and heads back to me. He slows enough so I can grasp him around the waist, and I cling on tight as his manta races after the others, now long gone into the darker blue. I turn my head to see Iona, imprisoned in her bulky diving gear, attempting to follow. The boat is a tiny silhouette above her.

And there's something else now: a growling sound that hums through the water, vibrating my skull.

27

Sam pushes open the door to the wheelhouse at the front of the yacht. It's also called the bridge and is where all the high-tech boat controls live with screens for navigation and whatever else. All three men now wear black wet suits and are staring at the sonar system, a dark screen with flashing dots. He's seen Tan and Teeth use it for tracking schools of fish.

"They've stopped. We are directly above them," says Nygard. Tan pulls on a lever, and the engine dies.

Sam swallows. "Shouldn't we be going back to the people on that small boat? One of them could be Iona—couldn't they? They might be in trouble."

Nygard turns and gives Sam a smile. "Sam, we'll check out the boat shortly. I'd like you to stay belowdecks for a couple of hours. We've got this under control." He pauses and dips his chin to meet Sam's eyes. "Remember Marisogen and your grandfather."

Sam shakes his head and points at the screen. "Got what under control? What are you looking at?"

Tan turns to Nygard. "Want me to lock him in his cabin? Be my pleasure."

Nygard looks thoughtful, and when he doesn't say no, Sam feels tingles of fear run up and down his spine. He knows for sure now that he made a huge mistake coming here, bringing this man here. Those three people out on the boat must be who Nygard has been looking for all this time, but now he isn't interested. It makes no sense.

Tan takes a step toward Sam with raised eyebrows and when Sam jumps back, he smirks. Sam blinks at Nygard. Isn't he going to say anything when the guy is threatening him? But the smile on Nygard's face is fixed, and although he is looking at Sam, it's like he sees straight through him.

Sam holds up both hands. "Fine. I'll stay out of your way," he says.

He backs out of the wheelhouse and through the cabin behind it. He glances down at the steps leading to his cabin. Whatever they are all up to, Nygard doesn't want Sam to see it, which means it is nothing good. At the stern of the boat Teeth opens a box containing harpoons and nets. Sam ducks and waits for him to choose a selection of hunting gear and pass around the other side of the cabin. Sam steps outside, flattens himself against the outside wall, and raises the binoculars. He locates the small boat. Now the girl is alone again—the two scuba divers who were with her are gone.

A splash in the water. Sam darts to the corner of the cabin to peer around. Teeth is overboard now, fully kitted in his scuba gear and with two harpoons at his back. He touches his hand on his head to show he's OK. Nygard and Tan are also kitting up next to the wheelhouse door at the far end of the yacht. Teeth tips forward in the water and disappears with a flash of flipper.

Sam tucks back around the corner. What are they doing underwater with all those harpoons?

The urge to get away is overwhelming, but there is nowhere to go.

Except one place, but that's . . . nuts.

Back in the cabin, Sam skips down the stairs belowdecks, stuffs his few belongings into his dry bag, and sneaks back up the stairs. His heart pulses in his throat. What is he doing?

He stares once more through the binoculars. The girl is still there on the boat, crouching down to look over the side.

Sam grabs a life buoy from a hook by the ladder at the stern of the yacht. He'll tow it behind him in case he gets a cramp or something. It is silent on board. All three men must now be beneath the water. He's never seen Nygard scuba dive before.

The feeling in Sam's stomach is more like a flock of trapped birds than butterflies. He climbs down the steel ladder and slides into the water. The sun is low in the sky, but he'll definitely get to her before sunset. He has to.

The sea is cool, not cold, but the girl's boat is farther than it looked. If she decides to sail away, he'll be alone in the middle of the atoll, too far from any of the islands, and he can't imagine Nygard will send a rescue party. He forces himself on, wishing he'd put more effort into swim training rather than obsessing about bikes. His shoulders burn with the effort, but he closes in on her slowly. He changes to breaststroke and tries not to think about the dark depths below him and what could be lurking down there. Finally he swims the last few meters to her boat and grabs on to one of the hulls. He rests his head on his arm, coughing and panting.

The girl glares down at him, machete drawn. She has an oval face with a slim nose and a wide mouth. The muscles on her arms gleam, and she looks like she knows how to use a weapon.

"Hey. I'm Sam," he says between gasped breaths. "I came

here to try to find some people. Aster and Poppy and their aunt, Iona."

The girl's eyes widen in surprise, then narrow suspiciously. "You came from that yacht."

"There's a doctor. I was with him, kind of, but . . . I'm not with him anymore."

The girl squares her shoulders and raises her chin.

"What doctor?" she says.

"It's a doctor who was treating my granda at a hospital in Gisborne, New Zealand. He also worked at a camp in the bush. East coast—"

"Wildhaven. It's Dr. Nygard," whispers the girl, pressing a fist to her lips.

"He has this drug, Marisogen, that was helping my granda, and he said he could make more if he found Iona, so I helped him find this place. But I . . . I think I made a big mistake."

She nods. "Huge mistake. Give me one reason why I should let you on board if you brought *him* here?" she says.

"Because I jumped off the shiny yacht and swam over here, probably through shark-infested waters, because I'm scared of him and know I shouldn't have brought him here. I want to help."

The girl purses her lips.

"Not being funny, but would it be OK to carry on this convo aboard? My dangling legs probably look like shark bait."

The girl sighs and steps back, lowering the machete. Sam hauls himself up and crawls to the center of the wooden boat. He flops down. It is so good to be out of the water.

"I'm Beti. Aster and Iona are down there. Somewhere," she says. She bites her lip to stop it trembling and gestures out toward the center of the atoll. "Aster fell in, and Iona went after her with spare scuba gear, but they haven't surfaced. The others from Wildhaven are underwater. They have . . ." She indicates her chest. "You have to see it to understand."

Sam frowns, trying to make sense of this. He remembers the dots Nygard was tracking on the sonar screen. "O-kay, are they all scuba diving?"

Beti shakes her head, exasperated. "You don't understand. Iona brought us here to get us away from Nygard."

"Why?" says Sam.

There's a long pause, then Beti meets his eyes, and hers are a rich brown, the whites reddened by tears. But her jaw clenches and her gaze is steady.

"He wants us. He wants our blood," says Beti.

Sam curses, apologizes, then curses again. Could it be their *blood* that Nygard needs for the Marisogen therapy? No. Way.

Beti frowns at him. "It's only been ten days. You didn't take long to find us."

Sam doesn't understand. She's only been here ten days?

Maybe she has nothing to do with Iona, Aster, and Poppy. No—she has to be.

"Beti—it was nine *months* ago I met those girls on the plane. I found the camp burned a week later and saw Nygard there poking around in the ashes. I found Poppy's phone on the beach. I'd nearly forgotten about it when the same guy turned up at my Granda's hospital bed and I recognized him."

Beti murmurs to herself. "The hibernation. They woke up, and we must have still been asleep in the container. For *nine months*. That is why they look so strange."

Beti gasps, hands at her face, eyes wide as she stares at the yacht.

"The four of us were in hibernation for nine months and they were living . . . under the sea?"

28

The manta ray Sea Boy and I are riding darts away from Iona so fast I can't see where we are going and can barely keep hold around his waist. They've left her behind, and I think I understand why. She *did* this to Sea Boy and the others. I grip tightly to my own forearms, hook my legs around his, and press my cheek between his shoulder blades. My mind speeds over the possibilities as quickly as the water speeds in through my mouth and out through the gills at my chest and neck. If Sea Boy and the others are from Wildhaven, then they must have been down here in the water longer than we were on land. Their clothes are ragged, and they are completely at home underwater. They've learned to ride *manta rays*.

Hibernation. We must have been in the pods longer than they were; it's the only answer.

After trusting that Poppy was on Halo West, then that she was in the container, I can't now believe she's one of these sea people. What if something happened to her?

My chest cramps with fear.

We've only been on the manta ray a few minutes when it slows abruptly, rearing up, wings flapping. Sea Boy drops free with me still wrapped around his back. I release him, kicking and circling my arms to orient myself. When we were moving, the water rushed through my gills, but now my chest rises and falls more slowly than it would normally to ease the heavy seawater in and out. I run my fingers over my chest. Unbelievable.

Slices of sunlight cut through the ever-moving surface far above, but the blue around us is dark. The manta ray has taken us deep. There is no sign of the other eight sea people; they traveled faster than we did. Sea Boy grips my arm and points down.

We are at the edge of the drop-off. About six meters below us is an uneven shelf.

I stare in disbelief as the shape resting on the ledge starts to make sense to me.

A shipwreck.

It is camouflaged against the backdrop, as if it's been dipped into a lumpy green-brown batter. It's the *Deep Retreat*. But it's so overgrown, it can't be; it hasn't been down there long enough to look like that. How long was I in hibernation?

I meet Sea Boy's eyes, questioning, but he is already pointing back at the surface, indicating his ear and shaking his head. He makes a cutting motion across his throat, then with his smooth dolphin kick, he shoots down the cliff face toward the shipwreck.

The low growl vibrates through my skull rather than my ears. It could be an engine, although I can't see anything on the surface. I look into the distance for Iona. If she is following alone, then she must be far behind us, and the rebreather cylinder lasts only four hours. My kit is on the boat, but Beti didn't learn to dive. She's on the boat, alone.

Sea Boy hovers above the wreck. I spin to face downward and circle my jaw, releasing the pressure in my face and ears as I sweep down to join him. It can't be safe for humans to swim this deep. Darkness passes over me, and I look up.

A block of shadow with a pointed end. It was a ship we've been hearing. Whoever is steering must somehow have tracked us here or detected the wreck with equipment. I can't tell from this deep how big the vessel is.

I kick powerfully toward Sea Boy, and he pulls me the last few meters down to the wreck, which is coated in a thick layer of barnacles, shellfish, and fuzzy weeds. Can Sea Boy and the others really be *living* here, inside the wreck of the *Deep Retreat*?

I had thought the light was colorless and ghostly at the container, but this is another level; the violet-blue orbs tied to Sea Boy's shoulders provide the only light. He gestures to an opening in the top deck. I look up. The shadow of the boat is directly over the shipwreck, and this feels like the last place we should be right now. I shake my head, and when I meet Sea Boy's eyes I see fear, but also determination—he feels he has no choice. And nor do I if there's any chance Poppy is inside this sunken ship. When Sea Boy swims inside, I am right behind him.

At first it seems pitch-dark, and I almost reach out for Sea Boy, but my eyes adjust. The water is cold in my lungs and tastes faintly metallic. We are in the cabin. The windows are dulled with algae and other sea life, but a dim light comes from more of the bioluminescent globes, which hang along the cabin walls. I turn. The door is wedged ajar, the same door I tried to wrench open, where I beat my fists as white mist billowed around me. This is the cabin where Iona released the gas, the last place I was with Poppy, holding her in my arms as she slumped into unconsciousness. My chest cramps. Sea Boy offers his hand, and I take it. We glide like ghosts above the rows of chairs where Poppy and I sat when we thought we were taking a day trip. Cool water floods through my gills, clearing my head. A red-and-white-spotted fish with tentacles—a cuttlefish, I think—shoots past us. Figures loom into sight at the end of the cabin. A circle of sea people gestures to each other with expansive arm movements, like a large-scale sign language.

They see me, fall still, and turn. I kick closer, searching for Poppy.

Doubt bubbles up.

Can they really be the kids from Wildhaven, or do I have this all wrong?

A small figure streams toward me, whirling the others out of the way.

Her hair splays around her face in narrow cords, pale at the ends.

I can't believe it.

I look into her dark, deep-set eyes.

Her cheekbones catch the violet light from the orbs at her shoulder. My sister.

She's alive. Nothing else matters—it is *Poppy.*

She reaches for me at the same moment I reach for her, and I dig my fingers into the warm muscles of her shoulders—muscles she didn't have before—making myself believe she is real. She grasps my jaw almost roughly and surveys my face, her brows low.

Her lips move. *You.*

I nod and feel my hot tears leak into the sea. I clasp her to me tight, and we spin, chests heaving, the warm water from our gills mingling.

I've got her. Now I need to get her out of here—

Clang.

A clash of metal against metal judders through the water. Poppy and I cling to each other as we stare up at the ceiling of the ship, then she breaks free of me and whips out a knife. Sea Boy darts forward, signaling for the others to gather around.

The sound again, as if the deck is being bashed with something.

Shiny silver rams through the clouded window at the side of the cabin, shattering the glass with a crackling sound like an ice cube dropped in water. I haul Poppy back by the shoulder, kicking out as a figure, bulky with scuba equipment, enters through the window at the same moment as glass breaks on the other side of the cabin. The diver regards me through the mask. His eyes are colorless down here, but at the surface they would be pale turquoise.

Nygard.

There are now two scuba divers, one either side of us. Another shadow looms at the door, blocking the way.

A boy has been caught around the neck. The weapons are wrenched out of his hands, and he is dragged kicking out of the window. I grip Poppy's shoulders more tightly, and another girl swims forward, her knife catching the light from the globe at her shoulder. I recognize her as the girl I saw doing yoga at Wildhaven. A flash of silver. The same metal harpoon that broke the window. Nygard has it across her neck and hauls her backward. The girl kicks but is powerless to escape, clutching the harpoon and cutting her hands on its sharp barbs.

I taste iron on my tongue. Her blood clouds the water.

Before anyone can move, the girl is wrenched out of the broken window. Poppy kicks free of me and spins to Sea Boy with an angry gesture. I try to get hold of her again, but she is too quick for me. She grabs the harpoon left by the first diver and shoots out of the window. When I follow, Sea Boy pulls me back by the waist, but I draw my machete, shaking my head. Our eyes connect with understanding. There's no way I will leave Poppy. He releases me and draws a black spine from behind his shoulder. When I swim out of the broken window of the shipwreck, he is right behind me.

Poppy is way above us already. The three divers are almost at the surface, along with the boy and the girl they've taken, now bundled in white nets and struggling. Poppy's legs thump powerfully; she is gaining on them.

I kick with all my strength. What is she playing at, facing them alone?

One of the divers floats free and spins to face her. *No.*

He pulls out a gun and aims at Poppy. My heart stops. He's so close. He'll kill her.

Something white shoots from the end of the diver's gun, and another net, peppered with small weights at the edges, spreads out to enclose Poppy. The net draws tight, forcing her into a flailing ball.

I kick harder. I won't let her go again.

29

The third diver aims his gun down at me, and I dart out of the way, crashing into Sea Boy as a net shoots past us, missing its mark. Poppy and the others have already been hauled aboard.

I consider allowing myself to be caught—at least I'll be with Poppy—but I can't rescue her if I'm just as trapped as she is. What will Nygard do with her? She's got *gills*, he can't just let her drown on the surface; maybe he has a tank or something on the boat.

My mind races as I hover, staring upward. Nygard wants us. Or at least our blood. Iona found all those samples; surely he won't be satisfied with only three of us now he knows the rest are down here.

The last diver slips off his flippers and climbs the rungs of the ladder at the back of the boat. I wait for the engine to start, to find out I'm wrong and I've lost Poppy again.

Silence.

They aren't leaving right away. We need to plan.

Sea Boy grasps my hand, and I allow him to guide me back to the wreck and down the side, then over a second drop-off. He sinks down, upright. This is now truly the dark pit at the center of the atoll. There must be a fissure in the sea rock because there's no sign of the bottom. The water around us is darkest navy, and it sucks at my body as if it wants to drink me down its cold throat and swallow me.

Sea Boy halts my descent by gripping my upper arms. I gape up at the distant surface above, like crumpled foil; I'm mesmerized by the depth. Poppy is all the way up there. He leads me through some fernlike coral into a disguised cave opening. All the sea people are huddled together, and their violet-blue bioluminescent globes illuminate a small cave.

My eyes dart around in dismay. We can't stay here. If Nygard found the atoll and then found us, he must have scanning equipment, sonar or radar, that can map underwater. But we can't escape him and leave, not without Poppy and the other two Wildhaven kids.

A figure appears at the mouth of the cave. It is another scuba diver, and this time the sea people are ready. They brandish knives, lengths of pipe, and sharp shards of rock and surge toward the diver at the same moment I recognize the gray suit and the white of the writing slate. I dart in front of them, blocking their way, my hands raised.

It's Iona.

The sea people whirl me aside as they surround her.

One boy jabs a spear inches from her face. Sea Boy hauls him back, and there's a struggle. The light is dim but catches on her silver-gray suit clearly now; they must realize who it is.

But these are the Wildhaven kids. The last time they saw Iona, she gassed them on the boat, and then somehow they ended up down here, with gills, hiding in the shipwreck. They've just seen three of their people captured, and although they know Iona and Nygard had a disagreement at the camp, they don't know the extent of it and could think they are now working together again. They might kill her and might kill me if I try to stop them. And then what will happen to Poppy?

Iona's hand shakes as she draws out a pen and fumbles with the writing slate. She pauses. What can she write that would explain any of this?

It is almost like she catches my thought as she looks straight at me. I touch my gills. If Iona knew about the gills, would she have taught me to scuba dive?

Iona offers us the pen and slate.

Sea Boy swims up to her, snatches up the slate, and scrawls on it, then points up. I read his words at an angle.

He took 3.

Sea Boy is holding back the questions he must have. He only needs to know if Iona can help. The others gather closer, weapons still drawn.

Iona reads what Sea Boy has written, then rubs it with her gloved hand. She writes something and turns it to show everyone.

I will help.

I see the steadiness of her eyes through the mask and remember the puffer fish nest in the lagoon. The huge complicated pattern made by the tiny fish. Nothing is impossible to Iona. We have a better chance against Dr. Nygard with Iona here.

But the sea people don't trust her.

There is shifting in the water, more angry gestures. A group starts to close in on her.

Iona strips off her diving mask and removes the regulator from her mouth. The sea people fall back, looking at each other, confused.

She unclips the rebreather unit at the chest and waist, shrugging herself free so the equipment floats behind her. I swim forward and meet my aunt's eyes, but I don't touch her. Her hands curl into fists, and her eyes widen as she runs short of oxygen. I know that feeling far too well. But Iona doesn't wait like I did; she witnessed this happening to me, and she knows.

Words can't convince the Wildhaven candidates that she is on their side. But maybe this can. She said she tested the treatment on herself first. Whatever has been done to us has also been done to her.

Iona's whole body trembles as she pushes aside the gray material of her swimsuit to watch her gills open to the sea.

30

The sun sets, and the yacht doesn't move. The only lights are in the wheelhouse. Beti and Sam sit in the canoe in silence, taking turns with the binoculars. Beti offers him some warm water from a foil bottle, then looks at him sideways. Sam gives her a tight smile. Even though he's on a tiny boat with a stranger, exposed in the middle of nowhere, he feels more relaxed with Beti than he ever did on Nygard's yacht.

Sam has been expecting Nygard to notice he's gone, to

remember the small boat is there and come for them. But Sam isn't important to the doctor. In fact he suspects he's probably expendable.

When Nygard and his cronies hoisted the nets on board with three people struggling inside them, Sam and Beti took turns watching through the binoculars, helpless. He couldn't believe he was seeing people dragged up from the ocean like fish with no sign of scuba gear. Beti is almost as shocked as he is; she describes over and over what she saw earlier, how they rose from the water on the backs of huge fish, how they had lines across the tops of their chest for breathing.

Beti told him that Iona Wright had put the teenagers from the camp into hibernation on the seabed in order to cure them of a cancer gene and that most of them woke early and can now breathe underwater. He would have thought she was delusional if it weren't for the research he'd carried out on Iona and Nygard. Sam and Beti have pooled together what they know. Sam described the papers Iona wrote on hibernation and cancer-resistant animals. Seems Nygard decided he needed the kids' blood for the mysterious Marisogen he was trialing with Granda. So Nygard and Iona fell out. Big time.

Sam wishes he had the internet now so he could research how a geneticist could use blood to make a drug.

Beti interrupts his thoughts. "You were on board. Any idea how we could damage the yacht?"

Sam meets her eyes. "No clue, sorry. And they're really well armed." They give each other weak smiles.

"They haven't left yet because they want to capture more of them—of us. Don't they?" says Beti.

Sam sighs.

"Do you know anything that could help stop them?" says Beti. When he meets her eyes, they are so hopeful and expectant, he really wishes he did. He suddenly remembers the blog post he found about Nygard.

"I don't think it will help, but I read this thing. When Nygard was young he told people he had found a prehistoric mermaid, but then he said it was a hoax."

They stare at each other for a long moment.

"And now there's a load of people living beneath the sea, breathing underwater," says Beti.

He nods and stares back out at the yacht. "Not actually helpful now though, is it?"

Beti shakes her head and stands, hand on hips, the canoe rocking.

Before she says anything, Sam knows she's going to go. And if she's going, he's going with her.

Now the moon is nearly full, shining a pale gold path across the calm ocean. Sam and Beti row the sailing canoe as close as they dare to the gleaming white yacht, dipping their paddles carefully to make as little noise as possible. They swim the last stretch through inky waters, where Sam's legs kick out in jerky spasms of fear. He has never much liked being in deep water without a surfboard to hang on to, even in daylight.

The yacht looms above them. They haven't been spotted; no flashlights are sweeping the water. Beti and Sam wait. When they are sure there is no sign of movement on deck, they swim to the ladder. A light shines from the wheelhouse, but the windows farther back remain dark. Beti reaches the ladder first and turns, her eyes liquid in the moonlight.

"We'll try not to get ourselves killed, right?" Sam whispers.

Beti smiles. She has a gap between her front teeth. "Good idea."

She climbs up, waits for Sam to do the same, and they crouch together, dripping, behind the trunk that Sam knows contains weapons. No movement, so Sam peers around the box. The deck at the back of the boat is empty.

Beti edges toward the door at the back of the cabin. Sam follows, although nothing about sneaking back onto Nygard's yacht in the dark is remotely sensible. They open the door and wait for a moment. There's a low hum of voices coming from the wheelhouse at the far end, and a rim of light shines around the edge of the door. Sam has the urge to get closer, to try to hear what they are saying. But there's another sound, muffled.

Beti thumps him on the arm, and he turns to see a figure lying bundled on the sofa to his left, eyes wide open, a gag tight across her mouth. There's another on the other side of the cabin, a boy. Both are in rags, their hair matted, wildness in their eyes. They are bound at the ankles and wrists with orange rope. Beti darts over to the girl and makes an exaggerated *shhhh* sign, finger to her lips, then snips away the gag. The girl's intake of breath seems too loud, and Sam glances nervously at the wheelhouse door. When Beti begins to saw at the girl's ropes, Sam does the same for the boy. There's no sign of the third prisoner. Beti leads them out of the cabin. Sam follows, and they stop still, crouching on the back deck. They can still hear voices coming from the wheelhouse, but by some miracle, they haven't been detected. The boy and the girl shoot curious looks at Sam, then both grasp Beti in a tight hug, only for a second but with an intensity that shows they know her well. They gesture to Beti's chest, and she shakes her head. Sam catches sight of the boy's chest in the moonlight and gasps. Four diagonal grooves on each side of his upper torso, highlighted by shadow. The girl has the same. Sam knows it's rude, but he can't look away and has to stop himself from leaning closer. Could those really be *gills*?

The girl beckons them in and whispers, her hands holding her chest and her voice slow and cracked. Her hand is coated with dark smudges. It looks like dried blood. She's injured, but she doesn't seem to notice it.

"They have Poppy."

"Where?" says Beti.

"Through the door in the front," says the boy. Sam follows his pointing finger. He means the door from the cabin through to the wheelhouse.

"You go to the others. We'll get her," says Beti.

The boy and girl nod and pad across the back deck, flinching as if expecting a blow from above. As they pass the equipment box, Sam opens the catch, and the boy meets Sam's eyes with a tight nod. The boy and girl each grab a bundle of vicious-looking metal harpoons, test the sharp ends on their thumbs, and nod at each other, arming themselves. They slip down the ladder and into the sea without glancing back. Sam peers over the rail and stares at the ripples. They are gone. Swimming. Underwater. The lines on their chests really were gills. He shakes his head, trying to make the truth settle into his brain. Beti searches through the rest of the weapons. Ropes. Long knives in black coverings. A couple of gun-shaped weapons, one with a white web of netting hanging from the end. Sam takes the other net gun and tucks it in the back of his waistband, feeling like he's playing at being James Bond while wearing board shorts.

But this isn't funny. Teeth and Tan are dangerous, and he knows now that Nygard is the most dangerous of them all.

Beti grabs a bundle of the equipment they aren't using and drops it overboard. Sam winces at the splash, but there's still no movement from the front of the yacht, so he scrapes up the last of the ropes and does the same—if these underwater people have friends below, they could use them.

Poppy is inside with Nygard. Sam feels a vein pulse at his temple. Why has he separated the kid from the others? Maybe he's already taking blood from her. Sam brought Nygard here, so it's his responsibility to rescue her, but there's no time to come up with a plan. Beti is already making her way back through the cabin, and he shadows her, treading more carefully as they get closer. Sam grips the hilt of the knife tight.

A hand across his mouth, a hiss in his ear: "Shhhhhh." He stumbles backward into a solid wall of person. Beti whispers, "Iona!"

Something cold presses against his neck.

"Iona. This is Sam—he's helping."

The woman releases him, and he props himself up against the wall, hand at his neck as he realizes the coldness he felt there was the knife in her hand. Iona is as tall as he is and has short black hair. Her dark eyes are heavily shadowed but still glint brightly against her brown skin. She wears the same gray suit as Beti.

Her chest. The top of her chest above the swimsuit has the dents in her skin that he saw on the boy and girl. The *gills*. He drags his eyes back up to her face. She is one of them.

"Poppy is inside. With Nygard," says Beti.

Iona nods and leans forward. "You two go, now. I'll talk to Nygard, get Poppy."

Beti opens her mouth, but Iona holds both her shoulders. "Go. I mean it."

Beti nods. Iona watches as they tiptoe out of the cabin. They turn, and she makes a shooing gesture. Then she opens the door to the wheelhouse and steps inside. It sways shut behind her.

Beti grabs Sam's hand and squeezes it, and he's surprised by the feel of her warm skin, but in a good way.

"I can't leave them," she whispers. Sam shakes his head at her but at the same time remembers how those nets were hauled up the side of the yacht, the kids inside treated like cargo.

"You can go if you want," she says.

Yeah right. He gives her a withering look, squeezes her hand back, then drops it. They make their way back to the wheelhouse door. It swings ajar, and they flatten themselves against the wall on either side of it. Iona is talking to Nygard. Beti presses her finger to her lips. Sam gives her a sarcastic smile. *Obviously.*

"If you let us all go now, no one need ever know what you did. You can get on with your life."

Nygard releases an unpleasant laugh. "So you can claim my discovery as your own?"

"I'm not claiming anything, Jonathan. No one can ever know about what we did. I'll keep the candidates safe, then integrate them back into society when they are ready. These . . . genetic alterations can be hidden. We weren't to know the lungfish code would have this effect."

Now Nygard's laugh is almost genuine. "You still think this is down to your little animal-splicing plan? It didn't work, Iona! None of this is down to you."

"What are you talking about?"

"I did this. All of it. You simply provided the candidates to test it on."

Silence.

Sam's mouth drops open. The fossilized mermaid from the article.

Nygard raises his chin. "The animal DNA was ineffective, at least in deactivating the cancer gene, although the hibernation seems to have functioned. Luckily for you, as you could have killed them all."

"There was no luck involved; I tracked their metabolisms. I knew the hibernation was necessary for the therapy to work, and safe. I told you that."

Nygard smiles and shakes his head. "You still have no idea, do you?"

"Tell me," says Iona.

"When I was a student, I discovered an aquatic hominid fossil."

Silence. The waves slap against the side of the boat.

"Your prehistoric mermaid hoax?" Iona whispers.

"It was no hoax. I reported it, but when I realized the value of what I had, I covered it up. I retrieved fragments of her bone, and there was bone marrow inside. I extracted DNA. But the ice shelf shifted, and Maris became impossible to reach. I've worked on her DNA ever since. Until you destroyed the last samples of it that I had stored at the lab."

"Maris is the mermaid fossil? You *named* ancient remains, yet you treat living human children like specimens?"

"Come on, Iona. We both knew the Wildhaven kids were specimens."

Sam chews the inside of his cheek. Maris is the fossil. Marisogen, his granda's therapy.

"So you piggybacked on my trial," says Iona.

"You contacted *me*. You needed my help! Your trial had no effect, the cancer markers remained after the first batch of therapy. It was only once I added portions of Maris's code that the cancer genes were deactivated."

Sam tries to process what he is hearing. So Iona and Nygard were working together on this hibernation cancer cure, but Nygard secretly added the mermaid thing.

"But how could you know that it would work?" says Iona.

"I spotted similarities in Maris's DNA and that of the animals we were working with, and I hoped. I was never going to get another opportunity to test it like the one you provided at Wildhaven."

It's Nygard's turn to soften his tone. "Look. We are both overwrought, but we can still work together on this. I could never have predicted the physical changes would be so pronounced. The gills—they are fully aquatic—this is a miracle, Iona. Look at you! Think of the applications. The hibernation, the ability to breathe underwater. If you get them all aboard now, unharmed, we can work together on ways forward."

"Why do you even want them all? If it's DNA you need, then take some of my blood now and leave us."

Nygard speaks slowly, his European accent thickening, becoming clipped. "You don't understand, because you, Iona, have never had any vision. Their blood can be used to shrink existing tumors drastically. I ran a successful clinical trial, developed a therapy. I need an ongoing supply of blood, there are factors within it that I don't yet understand and that can't be replicated in the lab. This is vital work!"

Sam presses his ear so tight against the wall it hurts. Nygard is talking about Granda.

"You'd milk them of their blood like they were dairy cows. They aren't yours to—"

"And they aren't *yours* either!"

A scuffle, a stifled squawk. Sam tenses, meeting Beti's eyes. That must be Poppy. Nygard is threatening the kid.

Iona's voice shakes. "Let her go, Jonathan. You don't want to do this."

"I really don't. But I will. I need every single candidate on board. Now."

A stifled scream.

Beti's mouth hangs open as she raises her machete. Sam draws the net gun thing out of the waistband of his shorts and grasps his knife. Are Tan and Teeth in there too? He hasn't heard them.

Slam.

The whole boat judders, vibrations traveling through the floor and up through Sam's feet.

Slam.

Slam.

Slam.

The blows to the hull of the boat come in quick succession, all to one side. The boat tips crazily. Men's voices outside the cabin. A gunshot.

Beti brandishes a harpoon in one hand, her machete in the other. She nods at Sam, and they charge into the wheelhouse. Iona and Nygard are grappling, his back to them, and Sam catches the glint of a knife blade. Poppy rolls across the sloping floor, bound hand and foot. Beti whacks the back of Nygard's head with the hilt of her machete, and he slumps forward over the controls, releasing Iona. Sam saws through Poppy's ropes, and she rips off the gag. He pulls her to her feet.

He can't believe it's her. The last time he saw her she was waving goodbye to him at the airport. Now her hair is in long dreads and she's dressed in rags, but she has the same mischievous eyes. She glares at him in recognition. "You?"

"In the water, now. All of you," says Iona. She grabs Poppy and Beti and hauls them out of the wheelhouse door onto the front deck. Sam watches them leap over the railings, Beti's head turning at the last moment to check for him.

Sam takes the net gun from the back of his shorts and moves forward, staggering as the underwater assault continues to batter the hull.

More gunshots. *Crap. Steaming heaps of it.* Tan and Teeth stand on the rails, firing a net gun and some kind of dart gun—tranquilizers?—into the water below.

Slam.

Slam.

The kids in the sea are going to sink the yacht. Sam looks down at the net gun he's holding. He turns, searching for something else, and behind him is a red box on the wall of the cabin. Flare. He fumbles it open, takes aim at Teeth. Can't kill the guy. He points down, where his feet are on the first rail, and presses the trigger. He closes his eyes as the flare shoots out, and when he opens them, Teeth's shorts are on fire and Tan is grappling with him, slapping at his thighs.

Slam.

The boat heaves, and the men bundle into each other, hands sliding on the rails, and pitch over the side. *Slam.*

A grinding crunch. A rushing sound, and the deck judders as if in an earthquake. Sam turns. Nygard reels out of the wheelhouse, raising what Sam thinks is an automatic rifle. Sam freezes. *I brought this creep out here.*

Sam whips out the net gun with a shaking hand, takes aim, and fires. A white web of netting encloses Nygard, and he totters backward, down the steeply sloping deck of the boat.

Sam climbs the rail at the higher side of the deck. The yacht lists, rocking drunkenly. Before Sam drops into the water below, the last thing he sees is Nygard wrapped in the net, tumbling over the side.

31

I grip tight to Sea Boy's waist as the manta ray loops around the back of the sinking yacht. Moonlight only penetrates the top couple of meters of water, and despite the glowing globes attached to my shoulders, it is terrifyingly dark. We don't have long before the boat sinks, and my chest clenches with fear for Poppy.

The first part of the plan worked better than expected.

The manta rays and their riders battered the hull of the boat one after the other at full speed, the power of the fish's giant wings driving the metal pipes and other weapons gripped by their riders. The key to success was aiming at the exact same place each time, which we'd marked on the white hull with a big black cross from Iona's pen. After each hit, the manta rays swept under the ship, out of range of the nets and darts that rained down. A boy I remember as Dimi held our only flashlight, making sure each rider was out of the way before directing the next to attack, aiming the circle of light onto the cross on the hull so they would know where to hit.

Once the fiberglass of the hull was broken through, the pressure of the water quickly made the hole bigger, and we retreated away from the dangerous suction and turbulence of the sinking boat.

Now comes the most dangerous part. We need to climb on board the sinking yacht and find— A figure ahead, no manta ray. Moonlight illuminates her long cords of hair.

I release Sea Boy and strike out toward Poppy.

We cling to each other in the water, and then she grabs hold of my waist and propels me upward.

Poppy and I break the surface, and I gasp the light cool air into my lungs before I've even thought to hold a lungful of water. I remember Sea Boy when I first met him, diving underwater to breathe, and I tense, ready for the onslaught of pain. But Poppy grips my shoulders.

"It's OK. Turns out we can breathe both," she says.

I release the air I'm holding and look down at my gills. They have closed to shallow grooves in my chest. I can breathe sea and air, and so can Poppy. I am light-headed with the strangeness of it, and the strangeness of her, my brave little sister. She's so different and yet exactly the same.

The ship is now more than halfway sunk, bubbles boiling all around it.

"We need to get everyone away. It's dangerous," I say through wheezy breaths, surprised by the weightlessness of the air. "Can you gather them?"

She nods. "They are scared," Poppy says, her voice gruff. "They don't believe they can breathe air on the surface."

I grab Poppy into a tight hug, crushing my cheek against hers before I release her and dive. Sea Boy is below, eyes wide, stripes of moonlight dappling him. Poppy swims to him, tapping her chest, pointing upward and making a series of determined gestures. He nods, uncertain. She's the same Poppy all right. I feel a swell of pride at my plucky kid sister.

She clicks her teeth over and over. Sea Boy does the same, and my ears are pounded by answering clicks as the others start to stream toward us, circling around a meter below the surface on their manta rays.

Poppy and Sea Boy count them. My eyes flick from face to face. They aren't worried. Everyone must be accounted for—

Where is Iona?

I dive and edge closer to the sinking yacht. Only a couple of meters of the back deck remain above the surface—we have just minutes before the sea hauls it down forever. I sweep down deeper, scanning the water below with my flashlight. Poppy is beside me, and I mouth to her, hoping she can make it out in the dim light of her violet globes.

Iona.

Her eyes follow my lips, and her mouth hangs open in understanding. She nods, and we dive together, swimming deeper than the now-descending yacht but still keeping our distance. The pressure is like giant hands crushing my skull, but Poppy continues down. The beam of my flashlight highlights a gray hand, a flash of netting. We swim toward it, now surrounded by inky black. The sinking ship is directly above us, blocking the moonlight. I follow the beam and catch sight of Iona for long enough to see that she is way below us and is grappling with a man wrapped in the same pale netting that caught Poppy.

I swing my flashlight around, but all it highlights are clouds of bubbles, and I've lost them. There—the man is limp and drifting free of her. Nygard's pale eyes are open, lifeless. Iona sees us, illuminated by our globes. She shakes her head, frantically pointing upward at the mass of the sinking yacht, accompanied by fat globules of escaping air and clouds of smaller bubbles, only meters above her.

Why isn't Iona swimming away—escaping? Poppy holds me back.

I manage to hold the flashlight steady as Iona holds my eyes with hers. My gaze slips downward. The hilt of a knife protrudes from between the first and second gill slits on her chest. Billows of murk glow red in the flashlight beam like sunset storm clouds.

She's been stabbed.

It doesn't matter. Sea Boy healed me, so he can heal Iona.

I plead with her in my head.

Come on.

Reach. Kick. Breathe.

Never give up.

No matter what she has done, Iona is our family.

I shake free of Poppy and dart toward Iona, but it's too late—the ship is now plunging downward, and I'm dragged toward it. A fog of bubbles tickles the skin of my face and I try to kick away, but the suction is powerful. Then I am snatched backward, and Poppy's arm winds around my waist as she yanks me up diagonally, away from the ship as the last big pockets of air escape and it dips its nose downward and plummets. My sister and I hang there, clinging to each other, kicking against the suction, as we watch the yacht, Dr. Nygard, and our aunt Iona being swallowed by the dark heart of the atoll.

Quivering waters fall calm. The moon creates a single shattered star in the surface far above, drawing my sister and me upward.

PART FIVE
AFLOAT

32

Sam and Beti watch from the back of the sailing canoe at a safe distance as the yacht lists to the side, then dips. Finally it tips forward, and the last part to be engulfed is the steel ladder they climbed up only a little while before. Sam crouches, wondering if he should dive in and help, but he figures the guys riding giant fish and breathing underwater probably don't need his help. The surface bubbles like a boiling pot, but no one breaks it. Sam licks his lips. Could the sinking yacht have created some sort of vortex and they've all been sucked down with it?

"Hey," a cracked voice calls out. Sam scans the black water, and there she is, Poppy and another girl next to her, hair bundled on top of her head, curls clinging to her neck. Aster.

Beti leaps off the side of the boat into the water and hugs Aster tight.

"Aster! What happened? Nygard—is he . . . ?"

"Dead. And the other men are gone too; Sunee saw them tangled in the rigging as the boat went down. Beti . . ." She holds Beti at arm's length as the three of them tread water. "Sorry. Iona didn't make it."

Sam realizes his teeth are chattering and clamps them together. Nygard is gone, along with Tan and Teeth. Iona as well. People have *died* here, and he's stranded.

The three girls clasp each other tight, bobbing on the surface. Aster tells Beti about the others who are below, too scared to surface as they think the air will hurt them. The girl and boy he and Beti rescued seem to be called Mai and Darnell, and they are underwater, trying to communicate to the others that it is safe to surface.

Sam scans the water and makes out faint shapes. Dots of violet-blue light flicker and dart, and he sees a face looking up at him from below before vanishing into the depths.

This is . . . *insane*. He remembers what Iona and Nygard

were saying. These gills are a side effect of a genetic *cancer* preventative. Nygard really did find a fossil—there really were mermaids living on earth once. And now these guys seem to have some of their DNA.

When Sam looks back at the girls, Aster's chin is tilted up as she surveys him. Her eyelashes flicker.

"Sam?" she says.

She swims to the back of the boat and takes his hand as he hauls her up, then quickly drops it. She is dressed in the same gray suit as Beti, unzipped to her stomach, a swimsuit underneath, ragged at the neckline, revealing her gills. Gills. Sam tries not to gawk as the slices in her skin close to form furrows so slight he can barely see them. No one would even know . . . what she was.

"Really hoping you weren't with the maniac doctor out here to capture us for our blood," says Aster.

Sam winces. "I thought Nygard could cure my granda. I didn't know anything about what he had planned. But yeah—I did bring him here, and I'm really sorry. I guess I got a bit—out of my depth."

"Are you being funny?" says Aster.

Sam shakes his head as all three girls stare at him. Only Beti's lips twitch in amusement.

"Sam helped Beti rescue me and the others," says Poppy from the sea down below.

"And he marooned himself out here to help me," says Beti.

Aster shrugs and stares back over at the boiling sea, at the dying gasps of Nygard's yacht.

Sam breathes out and sways a little, feeling weak as it hits him. It's actually them, the sisters from the plane.

33

The sky is now royal blue, edging toward dawn. Poppy, Sea Boy, and the boy and girl who were captured, Darnell and Mai, eventually persuade all of the others to leave their mantas and enter the Halo West lagoon. They dart around, gesturing to each other, gazing up at the silvered surface through fearful eyes. They have seen us breathing air but refuse to try it. I am desperate to get them to the beach, out of the dark water and onto dry land, but I tell myself there is no rush, not now. Not anymore.

A tap on my shoulder. Sea Boy. He points toward the island, and I swim with him. When the lagoon becomes so shallow we can touch the bottom with our hands, I push out the water from my chest and stand up. I watch my gills close, feeling their slim channels with my fingertips and wondering if I'll ever get used to them.

Sea Boy rises with a splash next to me and strides out onto the beach, shoulders hunched. His neck is corded with tension, his eyebrows high. Unlike when I first met him on the mangrove island, he has pushed the water out of his lungs. As his oxygen runs out, his desperation will set in. I know that feeling too well.

"All you have to do is inhale, exhale," I say, exaggerating my breaths like Mom used to when I had a panic attack. Like Poppy did—and probably will again.

Sea Boy watches my lips and clutches at his chest, but I take his hand and hold it tight. The gills on his chest are closed flat. He rolls back his shoulders and draws in a deep, whistling breath, chest rising, nostrils flaring, and then slumps as he breathes out. He finds the same rhythm as me, taking longer and deeper breaths. When Sea Boy straightens up to his full height, he's taller than I thought.

"Anyone would think you'd never breathed air before." As

the words leave my mouth, I remember people have died—Callum, my aunt—and that Sea Boy's been underwater for God knows how long. Might be too soon for a joke. But he grins.

"It has been a while," he says, his voice rumbling, gravelly. "I'm Talal."

"I'm Aster," I say, and I hold out my hand. He takes it.

"You told me. When you were trying your hardest to get eaten by a shark. And I remember you . . . from camp," he says, and coughs. He has a slight accent, Middle Eastern maybe.

I drop his hand as his words sink in. He knew who I was? Then he knew all along that I was Poppy's sister, how worried I was, how terrified she must have been. I feel heat in my cheeks.

"If you knew me, why didn't you try to explain what had happened, bring Poppy to me?"

He raises his eyebrows. "I *did* try to take you to Poppy, but you were with Iona. I couldn't bring the kid to you, couldn't risk taking her anywhere near Iona after what she did." He meets my eyes, and my anger fizzles out.

Sea Boy draws a few more breaths and continues: "You have to understand. When Iona found me, I was living in a tent camp in Turkey with thousands of other Syrian refugees. My father was already dying of cancer, so there was nothing more she could do for him. I had no one else. Iona said she could take me away from there to a good, safe place. All I had to do was agree to a medical trial to make sure I did not get cancer like my father.

And Wildhaven was good. But then there was the boat, and when I woke up here, she did not come. I continued to believe she would find us at the wreck, even when the others lost faith. It took a long time for me to accept that she'd experimented on us, lied to us . . . then left us."

A flash of desolation crosses his face like a cloud across the sun.

"But she did come back in the end. He didn't tell HER. He told the people he was with all this time." His voice croaks, and he winces as if talking is painful, shuts one eye . . .

And in that gesture, I know him.

The boy with the dark hair who was working on an animal skin at Wildhaven. Gray eyes under dark eyebrows and a goofy grin. Now he has a mane of hair, killer cheekbones, and a lot more shoulder. And the scar across his cheek and eye looks less obvious on dry land but helped disguise him underwater.

"I remember you. You *winked* at me," I say.

Sea Boy looks down, grimacing. "I was almost glad when you didn't recognize me, because at least you wouldn't remember that."

I blow out a long breath. I can't blame him for not telling Poppy he'd seen me, not after what he's been through, and what we've been through together.

"In my head I named you Sea Boy," I say.

"Sea Boy?" He raises one eyebrow. "Seriously? Sure I'm more of an Aquaman."

Behind him, Poppy supports another girl as she takes her first breaths, and relief sweeps over me. She's safe.

I grin, and Sea Boy—Talal—grins back, and then our smiles slide off at the same time. We collapse forward into each other, and I surprise myself by wrapping my arms tightly around his waist. He gathers me in, his chin pressing against the crown of my head, and we almost lose our balance yet still hang on. His hug makes my ribs creak, and when I squeeze back harder I feel the rumble of his laugh through my cheek on his chest—and my own laugh might turn to tears but it doesn't, not quite, not yet.

Then Poppy wades over and grabs Sea Boy's arm, pulling us apart and shooting me the best withering little sister look I've ever seen.

Two seventy-six.

That was what the timer read in the container on the seabed.

It meant *days*. Days when I was asleep—a hibernating animal in an underwater pod instead of a burrow—and Poppy and the others, we were all surviving underwater.

Around half the sea people have surfaced and are now gathered around the fire, sitting almost too close, warming their hands, mesmerized by the heat and light. It's dawn, but no one mentions sleep. Plenty of time for that.

Poppy sits cross-legged next to me, close enough that our knees touch, and the contact makes me sag with relief.

"Nine months," she says. "You do realize I'm twelve now."

Poppy is only a tiny bit taller than she was, but a lot stronger. She seems so capable. All the others are around five years older than her, but they treat her like an equal.

She lowers her voice. "What would Mom say about this, Ast?" she says. I look into the fire, and my throat tightens. But instead of bundling it up and shoving it away, I touch the memory of Mom's voice. It stings, but there's something bittersweet beyond the pain.

My throat is thick. "I know what she'd say. She'd say you might be twelve now, but you'd better remember I'm still your big sister. So you should do as I say, Popstar."

Poppy breaks into a smile that makes me want to laugh and cry at the same time. She nudges me with her shoulder. "Yeah right, Astronomer. As if," she says, and takes a sip of coconut water, closing her eyes with pleasure.

I did it. I spoke about Mom. I feel light, and heavy, and strange, and like I might need to count my breaths in a minute.

"So are you going to tell us what you've been up to without me?" I say. The others around the fire fall quiet, listening.

Poppy tugs at her long dreadlocks and takes another gulp of

coconut water before clearing her throat. I remember she's been communicating with homemade sign language for the last nine months.

"We washed up on the beach all rigged in Iona's crazy kits and coughing up blue jelly. Set up camp inland. Freak. Ing. Out. Searching for you, searching for Iona. We'd only been here a day when Jack was diving, fishing, and started to form gills. Something went wrong, and he breathed air. He choked. He . . . died."

Beti stifles a gasp. I forget that everyone at Wildhaven is her family.

"That must have been what happened to Callum, too," says Beti. "There were these gashes on his chest, so strange, long equal lines. Iona couldn't think what could have made them. I guess they were gills, but savage, not neat like yours . . ." She trails off.

Poppy takes another sip of coconut water.

"Later we worked out that it went wrong because they surfaced when the gills weren't ready, so they were open wounds, bleeding, not working. When it happened again to Suki, we agreed not to enter the water, keep our chests dry, but some of us already had these weird grooves in the same place, like pre-gills. Then the rainy season came, and we were soaked all the time and afraid any water would open up our chests and kill us. Talal's grooves were deepest. He ignored what we had agreed—as usual—and his gills opened underwater. This time, they worked. He stayed below, and soon we all joined him. We didn't think we could breathe on the surface *and* underwater, that it would kill us like the others."

"So you *chose* to live underwater?" I say.

"You didn't see Jack and Suki," says Sea Boy. "Living underwater was a better choice than dying."

I remember Callum and shiver.

"So *that's* why you were holding me down beneath the jellyfish?" I say to Sea Boy. "But I didn't have these grooves."

"No. But I knew you were one of us, Poppy's sister." He raises his wrist, showing the broken arc of my bite mark, now scabbed over. "Although this is all the thanks I got for attempting to save your life."

Poppy inspects his wrist, mouth open. "*You* did that? Way to go, sis."

I shake my head at her.

"It wasn't all bad, though. Living underneath," says Sea Boy.

"Oh yeah, I mean, mainly it was *good times*. Hiding on a shipwreck in the dark, eating raw seaweed, shellfish, crabs. Scared stiff of the surface," says Poppy.

Sea Boy pulls a face at Poppy and continues. "We harnessed the mantas and taught ourselves to make weapons and hunt. Once we found the phosphorescent algae and made the globes, things were a lot easier."

There's a moment of quiet broken only by the crackle of the fire. I see grim companionship in the look that passes between Sea Boy and my sister. I remember what he said, how he trusted Iona, believed she would come back. I can't begin to imagine how they all must have looked out for each other down there in the wreck, bonded by fear. I stare out to sea and picture the shipwreck, less than a kilometer away, resting on the ledge.

Darnell speaks up from the other side of the fire. "Iona told me what she planned that morning. It sounded insane, but she asked for my trust, and I gave it. I helped her with the container and hibernation pods, and we sank the boat after so there would be no sign."

I frown. "So why didn't you come back for us if you knew where the container was?"

Darnell chews his lip and looks across at Poppy, then into the fire. "I did. I saw your pods were still closed. Honestly? I thought you were probably dead. If you weren't and I interfered with the pods or the controls, I might kill you. So I didn't show anyone else. And I never went back."

I open my mouth to say more but close it again. Would I have done things differently if it had been me in his situation?

My mind pans out from the container, to the wreck, to the sinking of Nygard's yacht in the center of the atoll. Then farther out, to the whole atoll, to Halo West, Halo South, a tiny ring of land in a vast nothingness of blue.

The New Zealander, Sam, sits on the other side of the fire next to Beti. He twists his fingers in his blond hair, face serious as he listens, staring into the flames. He has blond stubble that suits him and seems to be wearing Beti's too-small T-shirt. She's next to him. He catches my eye and smiles, and it's a good smile. Nygard promised him that if he could find Iona, he could treat his granddad's cancer with this Marisogen. He had no idea that it would be made from our blood. Tomorrow I will check the equipment chest for the memory stick containing Iona's research, but I can't see what use it will be. No. I can't think like that. This has to all *mean* something.

I stand, my mind spinning.

"I'm going to sit by the lagoon for a bit," I say, and Poppy nods. I know she'll shift position so her eyes are on me. I don't want to let her out of my sight again either.

At the shoreline I dabble my toes in the warm lagoon.

I run my thumb along the closed gills across the tops of my ribs. They are barely noticeable even when not beneath clothing. I feel the four behind my ears, easily covered by hair.

Nygard is gone. The men he hired are gone. Iona is gone.

Sam is the only outsider who knows about us. He says his parents will start searching for him in a few days' time—they'll find his note and come here. We haven't discussed it, but we can easily hide from them or go back with them if we want to.

I believe Sam wouldn't give us away, even if he could find someone who would believe him.

Our protection is that we are impossible. You need to see us to believe.

Sam told me about the article he found, Nygard's hoax, and Poppy explained how he had admitted to genetically altering us with fossilized mermaid DNA.

A myth is real. Mermaids once existed, and that isn't even the biggest miracle here. We are.

Nygard took our blood for his cure, and he needed more if he was going to market it. To Iona we seemed to matter as people, yet she was also the one who started all this. She experimented on us with the hibernation genes, and when she did that, she gave Nygard the opportunity to use us. To make us into these half . . . mer-people. I almost laugh at the word. But it's true.

Iona believed she was saving us; she didn't understand that we weren't hers to save. But without Iona's plan to sink Nygard's yacht, we wouldn't be alive now. I guess my feelings about my aunt will always be conflicted. Right now I'm numb. I can't believe she's gone.

We can stay here on the atoll, safely unknown, living off the land and sea. But I won't hide forever, knowing I have a cancer cure in my blood, that there are people out there like Sam's granda who I could help. But if the wrong people find out where we are, *what* we are, we could be locked in a lab forever. I think again of Iona's memory stick.

An idea takes shape in my head.

The lab needs to belong to us.

Science and math were my best subjects at school. I picture Mom at the kitchen table, peering over my shoulder at my math homework and sucking in a sharp breath at the tough equations. "You're as clever as my sister, Iona. Don't you dare waste those smarts."

I surprise myself by smiling at the memory. Anger and grief are there too, hot and sour, but that's not all I feel when I think of Mom, not anymore.

I never tried as hard as I could at school, distracted by my swimming, then by Mom's illness.

Now I have a reason.

If we go back, we can wear high-necked tops and our hair down and no one will know what we are. Not *if* we go back—*when* we go back. Because there are things I have to do.

College, grad school, it's all a long way off. But I know I'm smart enough to at least try to become a scientist. Sam said that his granda has had an infection, but he could still live for years on regular chemo and possible drug trials. There might even be time for us to help him. I could work on a cancer cure for—everyone?

Reach. Kick. Breathe.

I'm listening now, Mom.

One day I'll find out what my body holds, the secret deep in my blood. But not yet. For now, my sister and I are exactly where we need to be.

The lagoon looks inky black from here, but I know if I dived in, moonlight would slice through the surface and my eyes would soon grow used to the dark. That was Maris's place, and it is our place now.

I turn to look up the beach. Sea Boy crouches next to Sam, who laughs at something he says. He prods the fire with his spear, sending up clouds of sparks, and when Poppy smacks his arm he grins and does it again.

I press my fingers to my wrist, and my pulse keeps time with the waves surging against the reef. Salt water pounds in my veins. The breathing sea.

ACKNOWLEDGMENTS

This book was supported by the Society of Authors' Authors Foundation grant.

Publishing my first ever story is way beyond a dream come true. My heartfelt thanks to the following people:

My agent, Laura Williams. You were the first to spot me and swooped in just when I needed you. You are honest, exacting, and tenacious, and I wouldn't be writing this without you.

My editor, Rachel Leyshon. You drilled to the heart of my story and helped me build it into the best it could be. I've learned so much that I will hold with me forever, thank you for believing I could do it.

My publisher, Barry Cunningham. Your creativity is legendary for good reason, and I still can't believe I've reaped the benefit of your detailed input. I am thrilled to have you champion my debut book.

Elinor Bagenal, I feel in the safest and most accomplished hands when it comes to getting this book out in the world. Kesia Lupo, you sent your fresh editorial eyes over the story just when it needed it. Claire McKenna, for your eagle-eyed copy-edit and asking all the right questions. Jazz Bartlett and Laura Smythe, for working so hard to spread the watery word.

Esther Waller, for making the production process so smooth, yet so exciting.

Rachel Hickman, for your design vision and editorial comments and for involving me in the cover design process.

Helen Crawford-White for giving my first book its first face in the UK. Your fabulous artwork has been admired by so many. I still can't stop looking at it.

The brilliant team at Scholastic USA who have welcomed my story with such enthusiasm, especially my editor, Sam Palazzi, my exacting copy editors, and the tireless production and publicity team. Special thanks for the new stunning cover art by Kevin Tong.

The other wonderful Chicken House authors who have answered my wobbly questions and thrown the doors of the coop open for me.

Megan, for reading from a New Zealander's point of view. Rachel Sweetingham, psychologist and dear friend, for your early advice and constant faith and cheerleading. Sophia and Dan for your nuanced sensitivity reads. Thanks for all your input; all mistakes are my own.

All my Twitter bookish friends, I'm afraid there are too many to name. I first met the YA community through Lucy Powrie's excellent #UKYAchat. Lucy, you are a support and inspiration to me. To Lorraine and Miriam for hosting

#ukmgchat and Emma for #ukteenchat. To all the bloggers and booksellers who champion reading and give their time and enthusiasm with such generosity. Louie and George, submission support buddies extraordinaire. Giles Paley-Phillips, Seaford writing buddy, for your advice and encouragement. The brilliant and lovely Sarah Harris for everything from edits to laughs, support, and friendship.

Mags, Emma, Lyann, Claire, Helen, Margaret, and Jude, who remained my friends despite being subject to early drafts; I salute you. Anna KP for being there through it all, trusting it would happen. To my long-suffering book club, who have either heard about my book or read it at various stages and still maintain enthusiasm, I suspect the wine helped. Jo S, who read at a critical time and arranged for my first two teen readers, Charlie and Amy. I am glad my book was more interesting than English homework.

To my brilliant uni crew, your response to hearing out of the blue that I was writing a book made me feel like I could do it. And yes, there will be a party.

Jo Hogan. First port of call, talented writer, searing editor, speed-reading critique partner, and treasured stalwart friend. You've had a huge impact on this story and made the whole journey less scary and more fun.

To my Sally, for all the sisterhood and hilarity, and

unnumbered kindnesses every day and forever. I'm glad my first ever criticism came from you, and no—I don't know what the giant octopus was doing there either.

All of my fabulous family. My beautiful kind Nan, who has nothing but faith in me. Mom, for a house of songs, making, and art, for showing me how to find something I loved doing and then do it to distraction. Dad, for my love of the sea, for all the adventures, the runs, and made-up stories, for believing I could do anything. My brother, Rob, for the bunk-bed daydreams that sparked my early imagination and for all the capers and scrapes; you told me to write the book and for once I listened. My sister, Kathryn, trusted first reader, sounding board, and example of extreme patience.

Aster. The first fictional character I've written since I was ten. Nearly everything changed in this book apart from you. I never expected us to get this far.

My sons, Edward and Oscar, I'm inspired by you every day. Yes, it is a real real book.

Bill. I couldn't have done this without you. You are my calm in the storm. Thank you. Love you, dove.

Reader. Thank you for sticking with me this far. It's all for you.